Photograph © Tom Soper

LISA THOMPSON

worked as a radio broadcast assistant first at the BBC and then for an independent production company making plays and comedy programmes. She grew up in Essex and now lives in Suffolk with her family.

The Goldfish Boy was one of the bestselling debuts of 2017 and was shortlisted for a number of prizes, including the Waterstones Children's Book Prize. Her stunning second book, *The Light Jar*, was chosen as the Children's Book of the Week in *The Times*, the *Guardian* and the *Observer* on publication, and *The Day I Was Erased* was Children's Book of the Week in *The Times*.

Other books by Lisa Thompson

The Goldfish Boy
The Light Jar
The Day I Was Erased
The Boy Who Fooled the World
The Magpie Riddle
The Rollercoaster Boy
The Treasure Hunters
The Mystery of the Forever Weekend

Published in the UK by Scholastic, 2025
Scholastic, Bosworth Avenue, Warwick, CV34 6UQ
Scholastic Ireland, 89E Lagan Road, Dublin Industrial Estate,
Glasnevin, Dublin, D11 HP5F

SCHOLASTIC and associated logos are trademarks and/or
registered trademarks of Scholastic Inc.

Text © Lisa Thompson, 2025
Cover and inside illustrations © Mike Lowery, 2025

The moral rights of the author and illustrator
have been asserted by them.

ISBN 978 0702 32265 5

A CIP catalogue record for this book
is available from the British Library.

All rights reserved.
This book is sold subject to the condition that it shall not, by way of trade or
otherwise, be lent, hired out or otherwise circulated in any form of binding
or cover other than that in which it is published. No part of this publication
may be reproduced, stored in a retrieval system, or transmitted in any form
or by any other means (electronic, mechanical, photocopying, recording or
otherwise), or used to train any artificial intelligence technologies without
prior written permission of Scholastic Limited. Subject to EU law, Scholastic
Limited expressly reserves this work from the text and data-mining exception.

Printed in the UK
Paper made from wood grown in sustainable forests
and other controlled sources.

10 9 8 7 6 5 4 3 2 1

This is a work of fiction. Any resemblance to actual people,
events or locales is entirely coincidental.

For safety or quality concerns:
UK: www.scholastic.co.uk/productinformation
EU: www.scholastic.ie/productinformation

www.scholastic.co.uk

For Kim

Chapter 1

Team Dog Walk

It's hard to keep any kind of secret from your neighbours when you live on a road like mine. Chestnut Close is a cul-de-sac, which means it's a dead-end street and all the houses stare at each other like bored kids in assembly. So if something out of the ordinary is going on, eventually everyone will know about it. Melody Bird, who lives at number three, always seems to hear the gossip before anyone else. But there was one thing going on that even she didn't know about. And that was: who was moving into number one?

Melody interrogated me while we were out walking our dogs. "Are you sure you haven't heard anything, Jake? The NOW LET board has been up for ages!"

"No, Melody," I said. "And like I've told you fifty billion times already, I really don't care."

Melody huffed. She picked a leaf from a bush and began to roll it up in her fingers. We were doing our usual circular walk round the edge of the graveyard that was tucked at the end of the alleyway that ran next to my house.

"Matthew lives on the close too. Why don't you grill him about it?" I said. Matthew was walking two steps behind. He always came with us, even though he didn't own a dog.

"That's true," said Melody, turning round. "What do you know about the new people going into number one, Matthew?"

"Absolutely nothing," said Matthew.

Melody groaned and began to tear the leaf she'd picked into pieces. Then we all had to stop while her dog, Frankie, made his way into some long grass for a sniff. Frankie is a dachshund and the grass was taller than he was, so all we could see was the white tip of his tail bobbing left and right.

"I hope whoever moves in isn't going to be noisy," said Matthew. "It'll be awful if they're noisy."

Melody looked at me and sniggered and I rolled my eyes. I sometimes think Matthew is turning into Mr Charles, his cranky old next-door neighbour who likes to moan. It was a warm autumn day but Matthew was wearing a thick hoodie and a jacket. A while back he had these weird fears about germs and being ill and stuff. He was seeing a therapist for a while, but I think he's been feeling better lately so he's stopped. I noticed he still liked to keep his skin covered, though. I was wearing a T-shirt and shorts, and I was really hot so Matthew must have been roasting.

"Hopefully there'll be a girl moving in," Melody continued. "I'm outnumbered with you two."

Me, Matthew and Melody are the only young people on Chestnut Close and we're all in the same year at school. Matthew and I were best friends in primary school, but he went off with some other kids when we started secondary, which was annoying. I guess I wasn't too nice to him back then, so that probably had a lot to do with it. Then, a couple of summers ago, a little kid went missing in our street. What happened kind of brought us together and we sorted out our issues and now we're mates again. As well as the three of us and our parents, there's a couple in their fifties, Kyle and Cameron, living between me and Matthew who's at number nine; Mr Charles, as I mentioned, who is probably in his seventies, at number eleven; and Old Nina – rumoured to be nearly a hundred – who lives in the Rectory. I cut Old Nina's lawn every week and, even though she's ancient, she's really nice.

Frankie eventually emerged from the long grass, had a shake and we carried on.

"Maybe the new neighbours will have a dog and they can come walking with us," Melody said with a smile. Both Matthew and I grunted in reply. Melody was always over-friendly like that. It was down to her that we did this daily dog walk together at all. I used to walk Wilson on my own, until one day I bumped into her and Frankie and, after that, she just started knocking for me, so I didn't have much choice. Matthew tagged along too, which was fine by me because, although he is the opposite of Melody and can be a bit quiet sometimes, which makes you wonder if he actually likes you, he's still my best friend. And when he's in a good mood and not worrying about stuff, Matthew can be really funny.

"Maybe it'll be an older couple who will keep themselves to themselves and don't go out much like

Old Nina," said Matthew. He tugged on the cuff of his jacket and folded his arms against his chest. He tapped his finger over and over on his arm, which was a habit I'd noticed him doing a lot lately. It made me wonder if his anxiety was getting bad again.

My dog, Wilson, was the next one to hold us up. We stopped while he sniffed at an old grey headstone. I looked around as the sunlight flickered through the canopy of orange leaves on to the graves. The graveyard is Melody's favourite place in the whole world and I used to tease her about it and say she was weird because she liked hanging out with dead people, but it was just a joke. She says the graveyard is full of beauty and history, and that the huge stone angels are works of art, rather than so creepy you dare not look at them in case their eyes move.

Wilson finished sniffing and bounded on ahead, pulling on his lead, and I pretended he was so strong I couldn't control him, which made Melody and Matthew snort with laughter. Wilson is a breed called a Bichon Frisé and he's small, white and very fluffy. Matthew once said he looked like a cloud on legs. If you looked up his breed on the internet, it would say that they are playful, affectionate, cheerful and sensitive – which is exactly what Wilson is like, especially the sensitive bit. Every time we walk he tries to play with Frankie, but Frankie is old and just sticks his pointed nose in the air and ignores him. I'm convinced Wilson gets upset about it. He's the perfect dog for me because I have allergies and he is hypoallergenic, which means I don't wheeze or get a rash if I'm near him.

We ambled down the alleyway, back towards Chestnut Close, with its six identical houses facing each other across the street. At the top is Old Nina's creepy house known as the Rectory. Her house dates back to Victorian times, and when I mowed her lawn last week, I found a dirty ring in the grass that I reckon could be really old. I showed it to her, but she said I could keep it and that it was probably just made of tin, so it doesn't look like I'm going to be rich or anything.

There was a *HONK, HONK, HONK* sound as we reached the pavement.

"Oh no. It sounds like it's practice time again," said Matthew.

Kyle from number seven was sitting in his lounge, playing his bassoon. He plays in an orchestra and travels the world. To be honest, I never knew a bassoon was a thing before Kyle and Cameron moved in a month ago. It looks a bit like a piece of plumbing to me, and it sounds like a honking goose through our living-room wall, but Melody's mum Claudia told her they sound better when the other instruments join in.

Kyle was concentrating on the sheet of music on a silver stand as *HONK, HONK, HONK* floated through the open window. He spotted us and stopped, lifting an arm to wave. We waved back.

"Mr Charles is enjoying it," said Matthew, smirking. "Look at him. He's almost dancing!"

Mr Charles lives on the other side of Matthew and he was outside sweeping the pavement and bobbing his head to the honk of the bassoon. It was his grandson who went missing that summer: a little toddler called Teddy who was staying along with his older sister Casey.

"Do you two want to come over?" asked Melody. "We can make some brownies if you like."

"I can't. I'm going out," said Matthew, checking his watch.

"Are you? Where?" said Melody.

Matthew stared at the pavement. "Nowhere you'd be interested in, Melody Bird," he said shortly.

Melody raised her eyebrows at me.

Matthew had been acting a bit odd lately. As well as the tapping on his arm, it was like he had some big secret he didn't want us to know about. Melody had noticed it too, by the face she was pulling.

She turned to me. "What about you, Jake? Want to do some baking?"

I shook my head. "Nah, you're all right."

"Are you sure? We can make them at yours instead."

"I said no, didn't I?" I snapped. I realized I'd been a bit rude so muttered, "Thanks, though."

Melody blew some air out of her cheeks. "Wow. Two rejections in one minute. That's a record!"

I smirked and Matthew smiled.

"Right, see you in the morning," said Matthew before hurrying across the road.

Melody took a step closer to me and spoke out of the side of her mouth. "He's been acting strange, don't you think?"

I shrugged. "Yeah. Maybe. I'll see you later," I said.

I didn't want to talk about whatever was going on with Matthew right now. After all, he wasn't the only one who had a secret.

Chapter 2

My Secret

When I got home from my dog walk with Melody and Matthew, I opened our front door and unclipped Wilson's lead before going to the kitchen. I let out a gasp. Mum was sitting on the floor by the fridge in her dressing gown!

"Mum? What are you doing?" I shouted.

"Oh, Jake. I'm sorry. I was looking for something for dinner but there isn't anything. I … I felt overwhelmed and had to sit."

I took her arm and helped her up and into a kitchen chair. Wilson went to his water bowl, then flopped in his basket, resting his head on the side as he watched us. Mum's skin felt cold, and she pulled the front of her dressing gown tighter. I wasn't sure what to do, so I put the kettle on.

Mum hadn't been right for a while now, and it wasn't the first time something like this had happened. A few years ago she was made redundant from her job in a pharmacy. She was OK to start with, but when no other jobs came up, she stopped going out and said she was tired all the time. All she seemed to want to do was sit and watch TV. Mum is usually really busy, even when she's not working, like decorating the house or going out with her friends, so me and my older brother, Leo, were a bit worried. But she went to see the doctor, who prescribed some tablets, and within a few weeks she had found a new job and was back to her old self. But this time, on top of being sad, she was doing odd things. And she hadn't made any attempts to see a doctor again.

I got a mug and dropped a teabag into it, then went to the fridge for the milk. There was still a little bit left in the carton, but Mum was right about the food. The fridge contained: a jar of pickle, some butter, a small chunk of cheese that had white furry stuff on it and a mouldy cucumber. She hadn't been shopping in ages so we'd just been eating soup or baked beans that I'd found in the cupboard.

"Have you had anything to eat today?" I asked.

Mum shook her head. I checked the bread bin. There was one slice left and I put it in the toaster. I'm not good at stuff like this. I just wanted my old mum back. I spotted her phone on the counter and picked it up, waving it at her.

"You should call the doctor, Mum," I said. "Remember when you felt sad before and they helped you?"

I held the phone out but she didn't take it from me.

"You've got to ask about my eczema cream too, remember? You don't want my skin getting bad again, do you?" I said.

"I'll call them in the morning," she said. Then she rubbed at her forehead like she had an itch she couldn't get rid of.

"How about I call Auntie Wendy? She could come and stay for a bit?" I said.

"No! Don't do that. She won't want to speak to me."

"Why? What happened, Mum?" I asked. But Mum just shook her head and said nothing.

I really liked Auntie Wendy. We'd been on

holiday with her to her caravan in the summer. I was expecting it to be boring, but it was really good fun – until Auntie Wendy dropped the bombshell that she was moving to Scotland after the summer. They had some kind of argument and then Auntie Wendy moved away. As far as I knew, they hadn't spoken since. Mum seemed pretty low after that, but I thought she would soon cheer up and it would blow over eventually. But then, last Monday, she came home from her shift at the supermarket and, instead of chatting with me while she cooked the dinner like she usually did, she went straight to bed. The next morning she slept through her alarm and I had to bang on her bedroom door to wake her up. And then, when I told her I'd run out of my cream from the doctor, she said she'd get me another prescription but didn't do anything about it. Which was really strange because Mum usually fusses over me because of my eczema and allergies. One evening we were watching TV when she turned to me and said, "Jake? Do you ever feel like you're on the outside of your head and looking in on yourself?" Her eyes looked watery.

I swallowed. I didn't like Mum saying weird things like that. It was scary.

"Of course I don't. That's a silly thing to say, Mum," I said, frowning. "Stop talking like that. All right?"

She nodded and said she was just tired and she was going to bed. The next morning I'd overheard her on the phone to her work saying that she was ill with the flu. My mum *never* tells lies. She'd told me she'd be fine after she'd had a rest, but that was days ago and she seemed to be getting worse. And everything that needed to be done around the house, like the washing and finding something for dinner, had suddenly become *my* job. My dad has never been part of my life, and since Leo moved out, it has just been the two of us. I thought about telling Matthew and Melody, but I felt embarrassed. For Mum, I guess. I didn't want anyone to see her like that. Not when she was doing crazy things like sitting on the kitchen floor.

I got a plate for Mum's toast and the butter from the fridge. There was just a scraping left.

"Why don't I get in touch with Leo, Mum?" I said. I hadn't always got on with my big brother, but he had messaged me a few times from Australia where he was working as a car mechanic. I think he was missing us.

"No! You can't worry him," Mum said, pulling on the cuffs of her dressing gown.

Leo left earlier in the year and although Mum had been happy that he'd found this amazing opportunity, I think it was then that she'd started to change. She ignored her friends' phone calls and didn't seem to talk so much to me, either. It was like her volume dial had been turned down. What with Leo going and Auntie Wendy moving I think she was feeling a bit lost. I'd even heard her muttering a few times that 'everyone kept leaving her'.

"Please don't tell anyone about this, will you, Jake?" said Mum. "If people get involved, then ... I'm worried about what might happen to you."

Happen to me? What was she talking about?

She wiped a tear from her cheek. "Jake? Promise me? You can't say anything. I don't want to lose you as well as Leo and Wendy."

"OK," I muttered. "But you have to call the doctor."

She nodded, slowly. "I'm too tired now. But I will," she said. She was looking right at me, but it was like her eyes weren't focusing properly. "I'm sorry, Jake," she said.

I hated her being like this. And I hated having to be in charge of everything instead of the other way round. I looked in the cupboards to see if we had any kind of spread to go on the toast but there wasn't anything.

"Actually, I think I'm going to go back to bed now," Mum said. My shoulders dropped as I watched her slowly get up and leave the room, just as the kettle switched off and the toast popped.

I met Matthew and Melody outside my house the next morning. We always walked to school together, which made going in a bit easier. I didn't like school much and I was counting down the days until the half-term holiday.

As we walked, Melody jabbered on about her timetable.

"I've got French first. Then science. I love Mr Turner, don't you? What have you got first period, Matthew?"

"Erm. Maths," said Matthew.

Melody looked at me next. I had no idea why our timetables were so interesting to her, but it was likely that she just wanted to talk about anything, even if it was boring stuff. Melody did like to chat.

"Art," I said. Art was one lesson I didn't mind too much. I liked drawing and the teacher had said I was a natural sculptor when I made a baby dragon out of clay. I secretly wondered if I could do something like that for a job one day. Maybe I could be a model-maker for a film set?

Melody carried on talking about what classes she had in the afternoon, and I zoned out.

The bell went a minute after we arrived. When I walked in to my form class, a boy called Jamie made an 'urgh' noise as I walked past his desk. I sat behind him and he spun round.

"OMG, Jake Bishop, what's going on with your neck? Have you been attacked by a tiger or something? Your neck is *actually* bleeding."

I pulled my shirt collar up a little, resisting the urge to scratch. I was having a bad flare-up. I was supposed to use the cream from the doctor every day to stop it from getting worse, but I hadn't for two weeks now.

"It's eczema," I muttered. I got my book out of my bag and sat down. Our form tutor, Ms McGovern, was promoting 'reading for pleasure', and last week we'd all borrowed a book from the school library. I'd chosen a graphic novel.

"Gross," muttered Jamie, before he turned back round.

I acted like nothing had happened and stared at the images in my book, ignoring Jamie whispering to Mateo beside him. Most people didn't make comments about my skin any more, but I guess it hadn't looked this bad for a while. My neck felt like it was on fire and every part of me wanted to scratch, but I gripped the book tightly and tried to block it out of my mind. Mateo turned round next.

"You're really allergic to stuff, aren't you, Jake?" he asked. "Didn't you get ill last term? Like from a peanut or something?"

I nodded. I'd had a bad allergic reaction in the spring and ended up in hospital.

Eventually Mateo turned back round, but the whispering carried on. There was a time when I'd shout at them to shut up and butt out of my business, but getting angry only got me in trouble, so nowadays I just kept my mouth shut. Besides. Right now I had bigger problems to deal with: the fridge was empty and the house was slowly turning into a pig-sty. And, more importantly, what was I going to do about Mum?

Chapter 3

Old Nina Needs a Hand

Did you know that if you leave leftover Weetabix in a bowl for longer than an hour it goes rock hard like cement? I'm learning boring stuff like this now that I'm having to do pretty much *everything* around the house.

I got home from school, dropped my bag in the hall and shouted, "I'm back!" up the stairs. "Did you call the doctor?" Silence. Perhaps Mum was asleep. It was all she seemed to do these days.

Before she was like this, if she wasn't at work, Mum would usually be waiting for me in the kitchen with a smile on her face and her hands round a mug of tea. I'd grab a bag of crisps and eat them while Mum asked about my day and told me what had been going on with her job at the supermarket. She always had a funny story about a customer or something. I really missed her, even though she was still here.

Wilson trotted along the hallway and I picked him up.

"At least you're pleased to see me, eh, Wilson?" I said as I ruffled his fluffy head. I carried him to the kitchen and put him down. My cereal bowl had been sitting on the kitchen counter for two days, so I put it in the sink with as many plates, mugs and pans that I could fit in there and turned on the hot tap. While I waited for it to fill, I stared out of the window at the washing I'd hung out that morning and groaned inwardly. I'd accidentally washed my white school shirts with some red socks and now they were a shade of candyfloss pink.

Our doorbell went and I turned off the tap. Wilson hurtled down the hallway, scrabbling up at the door. I picked him up again and tucked him under my arm.

"Hello, Jake."

Standing on our doorstep, holding a floral-patterned casserole dish, was Old Nina. She didn't leave her house much, so it was a surprise to see her.

"Hi, Nina," I said.

"This is for you," said Old Nina, holding out the dish. "It's a chicken casserole. I made too much, and I thought you might be able to make use of it."

She didn't make eye contact and kept her gaze lowered.

"Oh, right. Thanks," I said.

"And I wanted to check your mum was OK," said Old Nina, her eyes flicking to mine. "I noticed her car has been on the drive for a while. Not that I'm prying or anything."

I was pretty sure Old Nina had spotted me hanging out the pink shirts on the washing line this morning, too. You could see her top bedroom window from our garden, and I was sure I'd spied her curtain moving.

"Mum's got the flu," I said. I'd got to know Nina quite well from mowing her lawn each week. I felt bad lying to her.

"Oh, I'm sorry to hear that," she said. "I guess you're having to look after her, then?"

"Something like that," I muttered. Wilson started wriggling. I let him go and he trotted back down the hallway.

Old Nina and I both stood there, silent for a moment, and then I reached for the dish.

"Well, thanks for this," I said.

"I've put how to heat it up, right there on top," said Old Nina, pointing to a yellow Post-it note on the lid. It was covered in neat curly handwriting. At least I didn't have to worry about what we were going to have for dinner.

"I've also got a favour to ask, Jake," she said. "Rather than cut my grass this week, I wondered if you could move those old pieces of shed for me? They're a bit unsightly, so I was hoping you could put them round the side of the house and I'll get them collected. I want to get that corner all tidy. It's been overgrown and messy like that since my husband was alive."

I knew the pieces she meant. In the corner of her garden was a large pile of wood surrounded by tall weeds. It looked like an old shed had collapsed one day and been left there to rot. I imagined it would be a hard and dirty job.

"I guess so," I said, trying not to show how much I didn't want to do it.

Old Nina beamed. "Thank you, Jake. I'm sorry. I don't have anyone else to ask, you see." She looked a bit embarrassed and I felt bad for being so glum about it.

"That's all right," I mumbled. "I could come over after school tomorrow, I suppose."

"Wonderful. Thank you," said Old Nina, squeezing her hands together. "And if you need anything, just let me know, won't you?" Before she left, her eyes glanced towards the stairs and I had the feeling she knew I hadn't been entirely honest with her about Mum.

I went up to Mum's room to tell her that Old Nina had knocked, but she was asleep. I huffed, then went downstairs and studied the instructions on the casserole dish. Nina said to preheat the oven to 200 degrees, but I couldn't work out how to turn the oven on. There were so many dials and symbols, it didn't make sense. I knew that the newer houses on the close had identical kitchens so I messaged Melody and Matthew.

JAKE: HOW DO OUR OVENS WORK?

I could see that Melody was typing.

MELODY: Set the temperature and then twist the other dial to the picture that looks like a fan with a line at the top and the bottom. When the red light goes off that means it's ready to start cooking.

I studied the pictures on the oven and twisted the knobs. It worked!

MATTHEW: Are you cooking?!

JAKE: Mum has the flu so I'm doing dinner.

There was a long pause and I wondered if they'd be able to tell I was lying.

MELODY: What did Old Nina want, Jake? I saw her on your doorstep.

JAKE: Do you miss anything, Melody?!

MELODY: It's called being observant, Jake!

JAKE: I call it being nosy.

She went quiet then and I felt guilty. I was quite mean to her back when things were bad between me and Matthew. She always seemed to be hanging around, trying to be friends with him and getting in the way. But now the three of us were good friends. It's funny how things can change like that. I guess we've all grown up a bit, too.

> JAKE: Nina asked me to move some old bits of shed in her garden, if you must know. Anyone want to help?!
>
> MATTHEW: Nope.
>
> MELODY: You're alright, ta.

I thought that would be their answer.

The red light on the oven had turned off so I put the casserole dish in, set an alarm on my phone for the time that Nina had said on the note, then went upstairs to my room.

As I changed out of my school uniform I spotted the small silver-coloured ring I'd found in Nina's garden a couple of weeks ago. It was quite dirty, and I used the sleeve of my school shirt to wipe it. It was a flat band with an intricate design etched round the outside. I was about to try it on when I saw there was something written on the inside. The print was tiny. I could make out a 'P' and a '7' but that was about it.

My phone pinged. It was a text from my brother, Leo.

LEO: All right?

He was typing another message so I waited.

LEO: Mum OK? She's not answering my texts.

Leo was one person I *could* tell what was going on, surely?

JAKE: Not really. She's gone funny like she did that other time. Do you remember when she was depressed?

LEO: Get her to go to the doctor again?

JAKE: Yeah. I'm trying.

LEO: Sorry, mate. Keep me posted?

I was relieved that at least someone else knew what was going on, but it wasn't like he could do much to help from the other side of the world.

I heard a car outside so I got up and looked out of my window. Melody's mum, Claudia, was pulling on to their driveway and I watched as Melody opened their front door, a big smile on her face. Claudia got out of the car and went over to her daughter, putting her arm round her shoulder before they went inside. I imagined them having a little chat about their days and what they'd be having for tea. I sighed and felt a hollowness inside me. Mum was only in the room next door, but right now it felt like she was a million miles away.

The way things were going, I might as well be on my own.

Chapter 4

Bad-Shirt Day

I woke the next morning with a jolt and the first thing that came into my mind was that I didn't have a school shirt to wear. The only clean ones were pink and probably damp as they were still hanging on the washing line. The one I'd worn yesterday, with the bloodstained collar, was crumpled on my bedroom floor. I grabbed it and went to the bathroom to inspect my neck. It was red raw from where I had been scratching it again in my sleep. When it was really bad I used to wear cotton gloves at night to stop my nails from breaking the skin, but I had no idea where they had got to. I sighed, then tried rubbing at the shirt collar while running it under the hot tap, but it made it worse. I'd just have to wear it and hope no one noticed.

I got dressed – the shirt now soaking wet as well as being covered in blood – then checked on Mum who was still sleeping. I went downstairs and fed Wilson, then let him out for a toilet. I ate a handful of cereal from the box as I watched him sniffing around the garden through the window. My shirts hung on the line like Wilson's pink tongue, dangling out the side of his mouth. I sighed, then called him back in. I looked around the messy kitchen, then stuffed some rubbish into the overflowing bin, forcing the lid shut. I didn't have time to empty it as I had to meet Matthew and Melody. I was going to call up a 'Bye' to Mum, but decided not to wake her. I opened the door and stepped out, instantly feeling myself relax a little. Getting out of the house was becoming more of a relief every day.

It was a warm autumn morning, which would have been nice usually, but heat made my eczema bad. It burned like pinpricks of fire on the backs of my knees and underneath my armpits. I took my blazer off, even though it meant the blood on my shirt was on show. Every fibre in my body wanted to scratch my skin. But I knew that would only make it worse, so I clenched my hands and counted to ten. I'd been taught to do this when I had to go to hospital for treatment a few years back. I decided if Mum hadn't called the doctor's today, then I'd ring them myself and ask for my cream. I had never called the doctor before, but it couldn't be that hard, could it? Maybe I could get an appointment for Mum at the same time?

"You're quiet this morning, Jake," said Melody. "Everything all right?"

"Yeah, why shouldn't it be?" I snapped.

I saw her notice the blood on my shirt and I think she was about to say something but Matthew was doing that weird thing again, tapping a finger against the sleeve of his blazer.

She spotted it too and looked at me. I knew we were wondering the same – if this new habit had something to do with his OCD. That's what the condition he has is called. The letters stand for Obsessive Compulsive Disorder. It's where you can get obsessed about something, like for Matthew it was about getting ill from germs, or you may want to keep doing something in a certain way, and then those feelings take over your life.

"Shall we do the dog walk when we get home?" said Melody brightly.

I groaned. "I can't. I've got to move that old shed for Nina," I said.

"Wilson should get a walk at least once a day you know, Jake," said Melody.

"Yes, I know that," I snapped. "He can come with me and have a run around Nina's garden. He likes it there." He also likes the fact that Nina always gives him a biscuit when we arrive.

"What about you, Matthew?" said Melody.

Matthew frowned and I noticed his cheeks flush a little. He was still tapping his finger on his arm. Maybe he couldn't stop himself from doing it?

"Me? I'm busy later," he said. Then he cleared his throat.

"Busy? Again? Doing what?" said Melody.

Matthew shrugged. "Nothing much," he said. "Oh, Jake? Mum said to ask if your mum is all right. She said she's texted her but not heard anything back. Didn't you say she's got the flu?"

"Erm. Yeah. She's in bed." Which was sort of the truth.

"More cooking for you tonight, then!" said Melody.

I glanced at her and she was watching me intently. I looked away.

*

School was OK, even though I got a few snide looks because of my shirt. A new teacher even stopped me in the corridor and asked me if I'd been in a fight. When I told her it was actually a skin condition she looked embarrassed and apologized, saying that I could talk to her anytime. I just grunted at her and carried on to my lesson.

When I got home, I was pretty certain Mum hadn't been out of bed all day. Wilson was scratching at the back door, desperate for a wee. I let him out and when he'd been, I stormed upstairs to Mum's bedroom. I was *not* happy about this. Mum was curled up in bed with her back to me.

"You can't lie in here all day, Mum," I said. "Wilson needed the toilet badly. He could have had an accident on the floor and then I would have to clean it up on top of everything else!"

I threw the curtains open, and Mum put her hand over her eyes.

"Jake, it's too bright. Keep them closed, please."

I stood there, staring at her. Why couldn't she just get up and go back to how she used to be?

"Have you rung the doctor?" I said. "I really need you to get my cream. My eczema is getting bad again, you know?"

"I'll do it tomorrow. I'm sure I'll feel better then," said Mum quietly.

"But you're getting worse, not better!" I said, almost shouting.

Mum put her hand out to me. "I will ring them tomorrow. I just … I'm just tired and my mind feels a bit fuzzy right now. And … I don't want to lose you as well." She began to cry silently.

Lose me? What was she talking about? My heart raced. Could I be taken away if Mum was really sick? I felt bad that she was getting upset.

"Don't cry," I said. "But please ring them. For me, OK?"

Mum sniffed and nodded. "I will. Thank you, Jake." She sat a bit more upright, and I could tell she was trying to make more effort. I was sure she'd keep to her word this time. And at least I didn't have to make any embarrassing phone calls.

"I've got to go and do a job for Old Nina in her garden," I said. "But I'll make you a cup of tea first if you like."

Mum managed a smile. "Thank you, Jake. You're a good boy."

I huffed. I didn't want to be good; I wanted my mum back.

Mum picked at the blanket on her bed. "It's funny how you used to be scared of Nina, isn't it, Jake? And now look at you, helping her out like this."

"Hmmm," I said. She was right about that. Old Nina used to really scare me. In fact, Matthew would probably say that I was terrified, but I wouldn't go that far…

Chapter 5

Melody's Scary Story

I'd never really had any birthday parties as a little kid, but when I turned eight, Mum said I could have a birthday sleepover in our old tent in the garden. I only had one friend back then so I knew exactly who I was going to invite – Matthew.

Mum put the tent up while I jumped around getting overexcited. I'd been looking forward to this for weeks and I couldn't believe the day was finally here.

"There you go," Mum said, standing back with a wooden mallet under her arm. "It looks great, doesn't it?"

The tent was very old and a bit saggy, and there

were holes dotted here and there, but to me it looked like a palace. "Brilliant!" I said, clapping my hands together.

Mum inflated two blow-up beds using a foot pump and squashed them into the tent and then rolled out two sleeping bags on top. She reversed out of the tent on all fours, making a funny beeping noise like lorries do when they go backwards. Her hair was all dishevelled as she laughed, and she secured it back with a clip.

"It's going to be a warm night, so you shouldn't be cold. Just don't lie on the grass, OK, Jake? You know it gives you a rash."

"Yes, Mum," I said.

Matthew arrived on time and held out an odd-shaped parcel wrapped in rainbow-striped paper. "Happy birthday, Jake," he muttered.

I grabbed the present and ripped the paper off. It was a foam glider plane. I'd always wanted one of those!

"Oh, wow! Thanks!" I said. "Let's go and try it out."

We ran to the garden and flew the plane across the grass.

"Let's try and get it into the tent!" suggested Matthew, who always had the best ideas. We took turns trying to fly it through the tent flaps and eventually I did it. We followed, diving inside and landing on our beds and giggling as we bounced about.

It wasn't long until we heard Mum's call: "Knock, knock! Dinner is here!"

We ate burgers and chips inside the tent, making each other laugh by putting chips under our top lips like fangs.

After dinner Mum crouched down by the tent door and took our plates away. "You have another visitor, Jake!" she said.

I peered out. Standing beside Mum and holding a massive red torch that was the size of a shoebox was the odd girl from over the road: Melody Bird. She annoys me sometimes now, but back then I couldn't stand her for muscling in on my friendship with Matthew.

"What's *she* doing here?!" I said.

"Jake! Don't be rude."

I noticed that Melody had a wrapped gift tucked under her arm. "OK. She can come in I suppose. But she is NOT sleeping here, all right?"

"Melody is only able to stay for an hour or so," said Mum. "Go on, love. In you go."

Melody dropped to her knees and crawled in, awkwardly carrying the present and the torch. She plonked herself on the end of my bed, which made me bounce into the air.

"Watch it! You'll burst my bed!" I yelled.

"Sorry, Jake. Happy birthday. Here's your present!" She thrust the gift towards me and I snatched it from her.

"You are not staying any longer than one hour, all right, Melody?" I snapped. "Isn't that right, Matthew?"

Matthew looked at me and shrugged. "I dunno," he said.

I ripped the paper from the present and studied what was inside. It looked like a very small telescope.

"What is it?" I said.

"It's a miniscope!" said Melody. "It's like a microscope but you can carry it around and look at things close up. Like a leaf in the garden or a ladybird or something."

I threw the miniscope on the bed.

"Terrific," I said sarcastically. I actually thought it was cool but I wasn't going to tell her that.

Melody began to click her torch on and off making the tent flash.

"Let me have a go," I said, taking the torch off her. I swirled it around the tent and then let Matthew try.

"Look, you can make patterns on the ceiling," said

Matthew. It was getting dark and the torch beam swooped around us, lighting up our faces as the beam passed by. Melody took the torch and put it under her chin. The bright light shone up her cheeks, making shadows under her eyes and turning her smiley face into something gruesome-looking.

"I AM A ZOMBIE!" she said, swaying from side to side.

"Ha! That's so funny!" said Matthew.

I laughed along too, but to be honest, seeing her face look different like that freaked me out a bit.

"I know what we should do. We should tell each other scary stories!" said Melody.

"Yeah!" said Matthew. "It'll be *really* dark soon, so it'll be properly frightening."

"Yeah, let's do it!" I said, trying to sound happy about it, although inside I couldn't think of anything worse.

"I'll go first!" said Melody. She cleared her throat, then put the torch back beneath her chin. "Once upon a time there was an old, old lady called Nina. She lived in a house right next door to a graveyard."

I swallowed. I already found Old Nina and her creepy house that backed on to the cemetery pretty scary.

"Each night, when everyone in the street had gone to bed, Old Nina would creep along her hallway, out of her big black front door and down through the dark, dark alleyway."

"W-what…? The alleyway next to my house?" I squeaked.

"Of course next to your house, Jake. It's in between your house and Nina's, isn't it?" snapped Matthew. "Go on, Melody. Carry on."

Melody brushed her long dark hair out of her eyes and repositioned her torch. "Old Nina's footsteps shuffled along the alleyway. Slowly, slowly she went until she reached … THE GRAVEYARD." She said that bit loudly and Matthew and I both jumped.

Matthew started giggling, like you do when you're nervous, but I chewed on my lip to try and stop myself from crying. I was getting really scared.

"Then, when she got to the graveyard, Old Nina did the most terrifying and strangest thing," said Melody. She took a long pause.

"Well? What did she do?" said Matthew.

I didn't want to know so I kept quiet, hoping she'd just make a silly joke and it would all be over. The whites of Melody's eyes seemed to be glowing from the light of her torch.

"When Old Nina reached the graveyard she could hear a strange scraping sound as the gravestones slowly shifted to one side. Then, one by one, the skeletons crept out from their resting places to ... DANCE!"

I jumped again but Matthew fell backwards, grabbing his stomach as he laughed. Melody wriggled at the bottom of my bed, a big grin on her face. The graveyard was just a few metres away from us and I thought I could hear something. Was it the scraping sound of cold, heavy gravestones moving?

"Old Nina danced with the skeletons, swaying this way and that. Their bones clanked and rattled."

My bottom lip trembled. Was that the sound of clinking bones that I could hear in the distance?

"They groaned and they moaned and—"

I couldn't bear it any longer.

"Shut up right now, Melody Bird!" I shouted.

"What?" said Melody, putting her torch down. "I haven't finished my story yet."

"I think it's good!" said Matthew. "Let her carry on, Jake."

"No. It's *my* birthday and I don't want to hear your rubbish story. I'm going to tell my mum about you and then you'll both have to go home right now."

I got up, but the tent was so cramped I stumbled and struggled to get to the flap.

"Why have I got to go home? I haven't done anything," said Matthew.

"Because you're being silly!" I said. "Just like Melody is!"

I fell over the blow-up beds and crawled out of the tent on my hands and knees on to the grass. I got up and quickly brushed my hands on my trousers. Then I ran inside, straight into my mum's arms where I burst into tears.

Chapter 6

The Rectory Garden

Wilson and I stood on the step of the Rectory and I stared up at the large black wooden door. I knew Nina was nice and certainly not someone who would dance with skeletons, but her house still gave me the creeps a bit. The paint on the door was peeling and it looked like sharp fingernails had been clawing at it to get in. I shuddered, then lifted the brass knocker and gave it a little tap. Through the window beside me was the dull orange glow of lamp. I was wondering if I should knock again when the door creaked open and Old Nina's soft pink downy face peered round the edge.

"Oh, hello, Jake," she said.

"Hi, Nina. Is it all right if Wilson comes again too?" I asked. Old Nina had a cat who wasn't keen on Wilson, and I didn't want him to frighten her off.

"Of course! Pepper is asleep upstairs," said Nina, reaching into a pocket of her skirt. "I've got a little something for Wilson right here." She took half a biscuit out and my dog snuffled it from her hand.

I'd been inside the Rectory a lot now, but it still felt like I was stepping back through time. There were red and black tiles on the hallway floor and a thick wooden banister that curled up the stairs. The wall of the hallway was decorated with a collection of framed photographs and I stopped to take a look at one. It was a picture of Old Nina standing under a tree with her husband Arthur. He was the local vicar, but he died years ago so I never met him. They were both very young in the photo and Nina's hair was brown rather than white. In her arms was a baby wrapped in a blanket and you could just see the top of his pale pink forehead and a few strands of wispy hair.

Old Nina turned back, seeing that I'd stopped.

"He was just a week old in that picture," she said, coming to stand beside me. "You know about my Michael, don't you?"

"Umm. Yes. I think so. Sorry," I said. I didn't want her to think I was being nosy or anything.

"It's fine, Jake. I don't mind talking about him. It keeps his memory alive, doesn't it?"

I shrugged, not knowing what to say. Many years ago, Old Nina's son Michael had gone for a swim in the sea when they were on holiday in Norfolk and didn't return. He was never found, so people thought he'd accidentally drowned.

Old Nina peered closely at the photographs.

I cleared my throat. "How old was he? Michael?" I asked.

"Just eleven," she said. "And I tell you, even though I'm old, and it happened many, many years ago, I miss him every single day."

There were tears in her eyes and I wondered how hard that must be to have a sadness that is so close that it takes just a second to make you cry.

"Let me show you something, Jake. Follow me," said Old Nina. She headed into the lounge at the front of the house, where I'd never been before. It was chock-full of ornaments and photos and bits and pieces, but it still felt quite cosy. There was an old electric heater standing in front of a large open fireplace with a green wing-backed armchair beside it. On the chair was a navy knitted blanket that was covered in cat fur and beside the chair was a small side table that was piled high with books, topped with a pair of glasses. Hanging above my head was a tarnished gold chandelier, the hanging pendants brown with dust. In the corner of the bay window was the lamp I'd seen from outside, glowing orange. Matthew had told me once that Nina kept the lamp on day and night in case Michael ever came back. It used to make me shiver whenever I saw it, but I've got used to it now.

"This is very special, Jake," said Old Nina, taking something from the mantlepiece. She was holding a silver trophy that was in the shape of a boy wearing swimming trunks in a diving position. "This was presented to Michael when he was just ten years old. He used to swim three times a week with the local club and his instructor said that he was the strongest swimmer he had ever seen. I don't think we ever saw him lose a race! He could have gone on to enter the Olympics one day."

She gave me the cold, heavy trophy and I read the shiny plaque on the front:

Awarded to Michael Fennell
Club Swimmer of 1982

"That's cool," I said.

Nina took the trophy from me, positioning it carefully in the middle of the mantlepiece.

"Everyone thinks he drowned, you know, Jake. But it just doesn't make sense to me," said Nina. "He was so strong. I'm sure he could have saved himself if he got into difficulty."

I wasn't so sure about that. You could be the best swimmer in the whole world, but the sea was powerful and unpredictable – anything could happen. Wilson sniffed around the bottom of the armchair, hoovering up some crumbs. On the shelves beside the fireplace were some small model aeroplanes on little wooden stands. They were the type you fixed together and painted, not toy ones.

"Those are good," I said, pointing.

"My husband used to spend hours making those. I've got some he never got round to making somewhere, still in their boxes. Would you like one if I can find them, Jake?"

"Oh, yes please!" I said. I'd always wanted to have a go at one of those, although I wasn't sure mine would be as neat.

"How's your mum doing, Jake? Is she on the mend?"

"No. Not really," I said.

I wished I could tell Old Nina what was going on. But I was worried about that comment Mum had made earlier about losing me. If she was really bad and had to go into hospital or something, what *would* happen to me? Leo and Auntie Wendy were the only family I had and they weren't around.

"Oh dear, Jake. I'm sorry. Flu can go on for a couple of weeks, can't it? But if there is anything I can do, just ask," said Old Nina.

I could think of a thousand things. We were running out of food; I needed my skin cream; I didn't know how to get blood out of a shirt; my mum needed to see a doctor – but I didn't say anything.

"Shall I start moving the shed now?" I said.

She smiled, then patted my hand. "That would be lovely. Thank you. There's a pair of old gardening gloves on the table outside. I'll get us some homemade lemonade. How does that sound?"

"Great!" I said.

I went through the kitchen and out of the back door and unclipped Wilson's lead. He shot off and had a good sniff around. I took my small sports kit bag off my shoulders that held my EpiPen and put it on the back of a chair. An EpiPen is a small medical device that I can use if I have a bad allergic reaction to anything. I always carry one with me: at school, on dog walks and here at Nina's. Putting the bag on my shoulders was as natural to me as putting on a jacket. Especially after the emergency reaction I'd had earlier this year.

The pair of gardening gloves were thick and heavy. I guessed they used to belong to her dead husband, which creeped me out a bit, but I put them on, trying not to grimace.

I went to the pile of wood and started with what looked like a door, dragging it across a wall of weeds on to the lawn. It was really heavy and left a scrape in the grass and I hoped Old Nina wouldn't be angry about that, but then I couldn't imagine her being angry about anything. I pushed the door into the dark, dingy area by the side of the house and went back for more. Some of the pieces were so damp and rotten that they fell apart in my hands making more pieces to shift, and I soon got fed up going back and forth. But Wilson was really enjoying himself, darting around and sniffing in all the corners of the garden with his tail wagging. In fact, he was probably getting more of a run-around than he usually did. There were some old wooden posts in among the pile that were awkward to move, and I had to walk backwards, dragging them. Wilson was sniffing around the last few bits, getting in my way.

"Wilson, get out of there!" I shouted.

Old Nina was watching from the kitchen window and laughing. I think she enjoyed it when we visited, and Wilson and I liked it too. She was almost becoming like a grandma to me, which was nice as my real grandparents died when I was a baby. I wouldn't have said that to her out loud though. It might have sounded a bit weird.

Finally, I got to the last wooden panel. This one was huge, and my arms were aching so much I wasn't sure I'd be able to move it. But I took a deep breath and heaved it across the garden with all my might, pushing it in with the other pieces.

I stood on the patio and took the gloves off, feeling a wave of satisfaction. I'd done it! It looked so much better, even though there was just dirt, weeds and a scraggly bush left. Old Nina came out to the patio with two tall glasses of lemonade. I wiped my forehead and sat down at her little metal table.

"My goodness, Jake. You've worked so hard! And it looked like Wilson wanted to help too."

My little dog had his head down, still scampering

about, his tail going round and round like a helicopter. He disappeared beneath the scraggly bush and the leaves shuddered.

Old Nina put her hand in a wide pocket on the front of her dress and took out a bundle of folded banknotes. "Here's some money for all your hard work," she said, putting it on the table.

My eyes nearly fell out of my head.

"This is too much!" I said. "I can't take all that!" It was three times the amount she gave me for cutting her grass.

"Of course you can. You worked really hard, and it wasn't a nice job. You deserve every penny."

She was probably right about that, but I still felt a bit bad as I put the money in my pocket.

A soft breeze cooled my face. I picked up the glass and the ice cubes rattled as I took a big gulp. It was sweet and bitter and possibly the best lemonade I'd ever drunk in my whole life. I sat back. Nina's garden was so peaceful and the harder things got with Mum, the more I was enjoying being here, away from my worries. For a moment I imagined living here with Wilson and all my problems vanishing in a heartbeat. But then I felt guilty for thinking like that and pushed the idea from my mind.

We sat and drank our lemonade and watched my silly little dog as he came out of the bush, panting, then dived straight back in again. I could have stayed there much longer, but I knew I had to get home and start thinking about dinner.

"I guess I'd better be going," I said. "Thank you for the money."

Old Nina nodded and smiled. "You're welcome, Jake. Thank you again for all your hard work."

I stood up and got Wilson's lead, giving it a little jingle.

"Come on, Wilson. Home time," I said. I could see the tip of his tail peeking out of the bush. "Wilson!" I said, a little more firmly this time. He still ignored me and I looked at Old Nina and rolled my eyes and she smiled. I went over to the bush and crouched down. I could see his little furry bottom and his tail wagging madly. He was digging and brown soil shot out from between his back legs.

"Wilson, stop that. We've got to go!" I put my hand into the bush and tried to grab his back end, but he twisted to one side. That's when I saw he had found something. It looked like a large white stone with some holes in it.

"Is everything all right, Jake?" called Nina.

"Yes. Wilson is just being silly," I said, still trying to grab him. "Wilson! Keep still!"

I decided that if I reached the thing he'd found and pulled it out he'd follow. I looked around for a stick, then crouched down and poked at the white object. I managed to push the stick into one of the dark holes, then I angled it so that I could lift it up and out of the bush. Wilson had worn himself out at last, and he came out covered in dirt and flopped on to the grass as he watched me.

"What is it you found, Wilson?" I said. "It's heavy!"

I eased the stick out and the white thing dropped off the end and rolled on to the lawn. I gasped as I stared at it.

"What is it, Jake? Have you found something?" said Old Nina, slowly standing up from her seat.

"Um. Yes. You could say that," I said.

Lying on Old Nina's lawn and staring at me with dark empty eyes was a human skull.

Chapter 7

Believe Me Now?

I straightened up and stared at the skull. Wilson came over and gave it a sniff.

"Get away from it, Wilson!" I said. "Come here!" I took a step forward and picked him up. I held him close. My legs were shaking.

"Are you all right, Jake? What's going on?" said Old Nina. She came over and stood next to me, peering at the object on the grass. "What's that?"

I looked at Old Nina. Melody's silly story about how she used to go to the graveyard to dance with the skeletons at night came flooding back. Maybe it was true and one had followed her home? I shook my head. No. That was ridiculous. It was just a story Melody had made up.

Nina bent forward to take a closer look, and then she turned to me, horror on her face.

"Is that…?" she began. "Is that what I think it is?"

I nodded.

"B-but," she stuttered, "what's it doing here, in my garden?"

"I–I don't know!" I said. "I guess when I moved the wood from the shed I disturbed something. Wilson must have smelled it. There might be a whole skeleton under there!"

Wilson gave the side of my face a big lick.

"Urgh, Wilson. Get off!!" I rubbed at my cheek.

"But I don't understand," said Nina. "How did it get there?"

"I don't know," I said. I stared at the old lady beside me. "Do you know who it is?"

She looked at me, her face crumpled in a frown. "No, of course not!" she said. She was holding a tissue, and she began to squeeze it, passing it between her hands. "What do we do, Jake? What do we do?"

"Nina. There's a skeleton in your back garden," I said. "You need to call the police!"

She began to pace back and forth, her eyes darting to the skull. It was hideous and I tried not to look at it.

"No, no, no," she said. "They'll come and dig up my garden and make a mess and ... and ... well, I don't want all that fuss."

I knew Nina was shy and private but I couldn't believe she didn't want to call 999! This was *really* serious.

"But you've got to! You can't just leave it there on the grass! They'll need to do an investigation and find out who it is."

Old Nina was still pacing, her cheeks flushed, the tissue getting smaller and smaller as she clenched her fists.

She shook her head. "They'll ruin my lawn. And you've worked so hard helping me tidy everything up. They'll have their loud sirens going and there'll be strangers asking me lots of questions. I don't like talking to people, Jake. I like things quiet and calm. Not loud and ... and ... busy."

I went towards her. Over her shoulder the skull was staring right at me.

"You've got to call them, Nina," I said.

Nina's face scrunched up and I was worried she

was going to start crying. I wasn't sure what I'd do if that happened. But then her eyes widened.

"I know what we'll do," she said. "We'll put it back where Wilson found it and forget it ever happened. No one needs to know. It can just be our secret, Jake."

Seeing the worry on her face made me wonder for a second if that might be possible. I didn't want her to be upset. But I knew that this was beyond keeping quiet.

"I'm sorry, Nina. We can't do that. Come on. Let's call them now, shall we?"

She took a deep breath and nodded, then followed me into the kitchen. Her phone was on the counter, and I picked it up and passed it to her. She gave me another pleading look, then took the phone and dialled 999.

"Police, please," she said. "I think … I think there's a skeleton in my garden."

The police said they'd send a patrol car over as soon as possible so I made her a cup of tea and settled her in the armchair.

"I've got to go home now," I said. "I need to give Wilson his dinner."

Old Nina nodded, her eyes wide with fear. She

wasn't someone who liked to interact with others much, so this was going to be hard for her.

"Thank you, Jake," she said. "What a palaver this is."

When I got home, I quickly fed Wilson, then grabbed my phone to message Matthew and Melody.

JAKE: YOU'LL NEVER GUESS WHAT I FOUND IN OLD NINA'S GARDEN!!!!

MATTHEW: Roses? Grass? A tree?

MELODY: Old lady pants on a washing line?

They thought they were so funny.

JAKE: Nope. A SKELETON!!

While they bombarded me with messages I ran upstairs. Mum would be stunned about what I'd found.

"Mum! You'll never guess what's just happened!" I said as I ran. I knocked on her bedroom door and rushed in about to blurt out my news. But the sight of Mum stopped me in my tracks. She was lying on her pillows, staring up at the ceiling. Underneath her eyes were dark, hollow circles and she looked paler than ever.

She turned her head towards me. "Oh, hello, Jake," she said. "Are you OK?"

For a moment I'd forgotten how unwell Mum was. And I wasn't sure she could handle the news of what I'd just found right now. "Yes. Erm. Wilson just ate his dinner slowly for a change. That's all," I said.

Mum nodded but didn't say anything as she stared back at the ceiling.

"Are you hungry?" I asked.

She gave a slight shake of her head. I tried to remember when she'd last eaten and decided I'd better make her something. I went downstairs and found half a loaf in the freezer and put a slice in the toaster. I read through Melody and Matthew's messages.

MATTHEW: What do you mean, a skeleton? Are you kidding?

MELODY: He's just messing about, Matty! Don't take any notice.

MATTHEW: What, like a corpse or something?

MELODY: He's lying, Matthew!

JAKE: I am not! There is an actual SKELETON in her garden. Well, a skull at least. I didn't look any further. But I guess the rest of it is there.

MATTHEW: For real?!!

MELODY: Wait for it! There's going to be a punchline any second now.

I thought I could hear a police siren in the distance. It reminded me of when Mr Charles's grandson, Teddy, went missing from the close last year. The police swooped in and there was a helicopter circling overhead for hours. But they wouldn't be needing a helicopter this time. I guessed the skeleton had been there for a while.

I went to the lounge and looked out of the window as a black-and-white patrol car pulled up outside the Rectory and two uniformed police officers stepped out. The door of Melody's house opened and she watched as the police walked up to the front door of the Rectory and knocked. I took out my phone and texted them both:

>JAKE: Believe me now?!

Chapter 8

Nosy Neighbours

It didn't take long for word to get around about the skull in the Rectory garden, and everyone descended on Matthew's house in the evening to discuss it. I knew this because he texted us.

MATTHEW: Everyone is in my house!!!! HELP!

Melody, Matthew and I were squashed into a corner of the conservatory drinking glasses of orange juice. Most of the conservatory was taken up with a pool table that Matthew's dad had bought a few years back. I don't think anyone actually used it – apart from their cat, Nigel, who was curled like a croissant in the middle.

The adults were mingling between the lounge and the kitchen, with someone going to the hallway window every now and then to check what was going on outside. I wished Mum was here too. She'd be the first to offer to help Matthew's parents, Brian and Sheila, make the hot drinks.

"Would anyone like a biscuit with their tea? Or a slice of cake?" said Matthew's mum, as she carried a tray of food around to everyone.

"It's not a party, Sheila!" said Brian. "I don't think we should act like we're celebrating or anything." He grabbed a slice of sponge cake from the tray and shoved half of it in his mouth anyway.

Sheila raised her eyebrows. "I'm not celebrating, Brian. We're all in shock, aren't we? I thought some sugar would do us good. Mr Charles? Would you like something?"

Mr Charles took a chocolate digestive biscuit and dunked it in his tea.

"What I want to know is how long it's been lying there. I mean, could it have been there a week? A month? Ten years?" he said. He lifted the soggy biscuit and quickly popped half into his mouth before it dropped into his tea.

"Ah, well. It's clearly been there some time. There was no rotting matter on it, was there, Jake?" asked Brian.

Suddenly every eye in the kitchen was staring towards me.

"No. Not that I saw. I only saw the skull."

"Oh, it doesn't bear thinking about!" said Kyle, shaking his head then sipping his tea.

"You didn't see any actual flesh, Jake?" said Brian.

"Brian! Do you have to?" said Sheila.

"I'm just working out the facts, Sheila. It takes a while for a body to decompose so if it was just bones, then it sounds like it has been there a while. Years, I'd imagine!" said Brian. "What did you tell the police, Jake?"

An officer called PC Campen, whom I remembered from when Mr Charles's grandson went missing, had knocked on my door and asked me a few questions. He asked what I was doing at Old Nina's house. What exactly had I found? Did Nina seem to know anything about the body? That kind of thing. He'd asked to speak to Mum too but when I said she was in bed with the flu he said he wouldn't worry her.

"I told the police Wilson had been digging around

under a bush and found a skull. He asked me if I'd touched anything. Which I hadn't," I said.

"That'll be because of the forensic investigation," said Melody. "If you had touched anything, they'd want to rule out your fingerprints."

"I saw a couple of people in those boiler suits taking things away in bags," said Kyle. "And the police have put tape round the front and back and there's an officer guarding the property!"

"Hmmm," said Brian. "It's a crime scene now."

"A crime? Oh my goodness," said Claudia. "Do you think that poor person was murdered then?"

Brian took another slice of cake from Sheila as she went past with the tray. "Well, I doubt someone dropped down dead in Nina's garden and she didn't notice, don't you, Claudia?"

Claudia raised her eyebrows and pursed her lips, shaking her head. "And on Chestnut Close too," she said.

"Have the police said who it is yet? Is it a man or woman?" said Sheila.

Again, everyone was looking at me as if I had inside information.

"No. They just said they'll be making enquiries," I said.

"They'll be checking the missing people database and if there is any ID on the body," said Melody, who seemed to be really getting into it.

"And how is Nina? Does anyone know if she is bearing up OK?" asked Kyle.

"I went round to check on her, but the police turned me away," said Claudia. "I could see them talking to her in the living room."

"She must be in shock," said Mr Charles. "She doesn't like any fuss."

"You're right. She really doesn't," said Sheila. "This will be horrendous for her. Absolutely horrendous."

Melody suddenly gasped loudly. And then a big wide grin spread across her face.

"Maybe it's her dead husband!" she said. "Maybe she poisoned him, putting something into his evening cocoa or into a meat pie, and then buried him in the back garden!"

"Melody! That's enough!" said Claudia. "Don't talk about Nina like that."

"No, no, no. There's no chance of that," said Mr Charles matter-of-factly. "Her husband died a while back in a hospice. Poor man."

Melody's face dropped and I think for a moment she was a bit disappointed.

The doorbell went and Brian hurried to answer. Sheila came over with the plate of cakes and biscuits.

"They're all nut-free, Jake," she said. Which I knew they would be. Because of my allergy Sheila and Brian never kept any nut products in the house, just in case I was coming over. I took a biscuit from the plate.

"How's your mum, Jake? Matthew said she's got the flu and is off work at the moment," she said.

"She's not great," I said.

"Flu can be awful," said Sheila, shaking her head.

"Let your mum know to text me if she needs anything, OK?" said Claudia.

"Same for me, Jake. You just need to ask," said Sheila kindly.

I nodded and sipped on my juice. I took a bite of my biscuit but I had a big lump in my throat so it was hard to swallow. I really wished Mum was here too.

Brian came back, followed by Cameron, Kyle's husband. He must have just arrived back from his work travels as he was carrying a suitcase.

"What in the world is going on and why is our road crawling with police?" he said, rushing over to Kyle.

"There's a skeleton buried in the back garden of the Rectory," said Kyle. "We've been living just metres away from a dead body! Can you believe it? Jake found it. Didn't you, Jake? Tell Cameron about the skull!"

Cameron let out a little gasp.

"Wilson found it really," I said quietly. I didn't like everyone looking at me. It made my face hot and the eczema on my neck was starting to itch.

"A skull? With empty eye sockets and teeth and everything?" said Cameron, his face aghast. Kyle put a hand on his arm.

I nodded. "Pretty much," I said.

There was silence and I imagined everyone was picturing what I'd found when Claudia changed the subject.

"I wonder who is going to move into number one," she said.

"Whoever it is I hope they're quiet. And they don't have loads of pesky kids running around," said Mr Charles. I think Mr Charles had already decided he wasn't going to like them, whoever they were.

He dunked what was left of his biscuit into his tea and this time it dropped out of his fingers and disappeared. "Oh bother," he said.

"I don't know, Mr Charles," said Sheila. "It'd be nice to have a young family on the close. But it's probably a good thing no one has arrived yet, anyway. Fancy moving into a new home and then suddenly the police are on the doorstep! Can you imagine? They might think one of us was a murderer or something! How ridiculous would that be?"

Everyone laughed, but Cameron cleared his throat. "Maybe not as ridiculous as you think," he said. He took a custard cream as Sheila passed and stuffed the whole thing in his mouth.

"What do you mean?" said Brian. "None of us have done anything wrong."

"*We* haven't, no," said Cameron. "But I saw Nina being bundled into a police car and driven away. It looks like she's been arrested. Maybe she's not as innocent as you all think she is!"

"Arrested? But that is absurd!" said Kyle.

"It's not, I'm afraid," said Brian. "To arrest a person you need to have reasonable suspicion that they did something bad. And finding a dead body in someone's back garden is reasonable suspicion enough, I guess."

Brian was usually right about most things so what he said must be true.

"Anyway," he continued, "it won't mean she's definitely going to be charged with murder. But they will certainly question her."

Everyone seemed to be considering the possibility that Old Nina had had something to do with this, but there was no way that was true. But still I had a very tiny bell ringing like an alarm in my head. So far I hadn't told anyone about how reluctant Nina had been about calling the police. Surely she'd just been in shock? She'd also tried to persuade me to rebury the skull and keep it a secret between the two of us. If I'd told the police that, then, yes, that probably would have sounded a bit suspicious.

But there was no way Old Nina was a murderer. Was there?

"That is the most outrageous thing I've ever heard," said Mr Charles. "I've known Nina for years. She wouldn't hurt a fly."

"I agree," said Sheila. "Nina is a sweet, private woman. She's absolutely lovely."

"Sheila is right. She's not capable of killing someone," said Brian. Then he frowned and looked up at everyone. "Is she?"

Cameron pursed his lips and raised his eyebrows so high that they nearly disappeared into his curly brown hair. "We don't really know what goes on behind closed doors, do we? And sometimes the biggest secrets of all are happening right under our very own noses."

Everyone's eyes darted around the room nervously. Then Matthew did a false cough and Melody and I looked at him and he nodded towards the back door. He wanted to talk in private so the three of us headed out into the garden.

"Is this for real?" said Matthew. "Old Nina? An actual murderer?"

Melody tapped her lip with her finger as she thought about it.

"Of course she isn't! There is no way it was her," I said. "I saw how shocked she was when we found the skull. She had no idea it was there."

"Are you sure?" said Melody. "What exactly happened immediately after Wilson dug up the skull?"

I traced the toe of my trainer along a patio slab as I remembered the moment I'd pulled the skull out with the stick.

"We were both stunned. I said she needed to call the police. She was a bit worried about doing that and—"

"A bit worried?" said Matthew. "Why would she be worried?"

"Yes! If she doesn't have anything to hide, then what's the issue?" said Melody. "Of course she had to call the police! Unless she was hiding something…"

"It wasn't like that!" I said. "You know what she's like. She just didn't want a lot of fuss. It's like your mum said, Matthew, she's a private person!"

"And you told the police all this?" said Melody.

I shook my head. "No. It didn't seem relevant," I said. "We found the skull. She called the police. End of. She only hesitated for a moment or so."

Melody folded her arms and she shared a knowing look with Matthew.

"Maybe there is a reason why she's so private. Maybe she's not shy at all. Maybe she's just hiding a huge secret. Like a dead body in her garden!" Melody had a huge grin on her face.

"Don't smile like that! It's not funny," I said. "Old Nina had nothing to do with that skeleton. All right? She wouldn't have asked me to clear that part of the garden if she knew there was a dead body there, would she?"

I noticed Matthew fold his arms too and begin to tap his index finger on the back of his arm again. Melody spotted it as well. He seemed miles away.

"Matthew?" I said.

His attention was jolted back to us. "I know what you're saying, Jake. But you must admit it's weird to have a dead body in your back garden and know nothing about it."

"Forget it. I'm going home," I said.

"Don't be like that, Jake," said Melody. "We're just looking at the facts."

I turned round. "The facts are that you are both wrong. OK? I'll see you tomorrow."

I stormed back into the conservatory, barging my way past Kyle and Cameron who were blocking the way, and then out through the front door.

Chapter 9

Helping With The Enquiries

There was a lot of activity outside the Rectory, and I watched as two people wearing hooded forensic suits came out of the front door carrying things in plastic bags, before going into the back of a van. Peeking over the top of Nina's fence along the alleyway was a white tent that had been erected over the area where Wilson found the skull. Poor Nina. This was exactly what she didn't want – her home swarming with people. A woman in grey trousers and jacket came down the front steps and

I waited for her at the end of the pathway by the police tape.

"Does she know you're going through her stuff?" I said.

The woman ducked under the tape and stood beside me on the pavement.

"Mrs Fennell has been arrested and is currently being questioned at a custody centre, which thereby gives us the power to search the property," she said. "And who might you be?"

"I live next door. I found the skeleton. Well, my dog did. Part of it, anyway," I said.

She looked at a small notepad in her hand. "Oh yes, Jake Bishop? I understand PC Campen took your statement earlier. I'm Pamela Thomas from the Criminal Investigation Department. Is there anything you want to add?"

"Only that it's nothing to do with her. Old Nina wouldn't hurt anyone so there was no need to arrest her. Just leave her alone!"

The woman sighed. "We're trying to establish what went on here. The skeleton was found on Mrs Fennell's property, so at this point, she is our main suspect."

I didn't like the way she was talking as if Nina was guilty.

"She didn't do it!" I shouted. "And you should put that lamp back on in her lounge window. It has to be kept on." I pointed towards the house and she turned to look.

"A lamp?" she said.

"Yes. It's important to her. She always has it on because … because her son died years ago. It's lit in his memory. So you've got to switch it back on. OK?"

She turned back to me and looked at her notepad. "No problem. I can arrange that. Her son died, you say? When was this?"

I shrugged. "I dunno. The 1980s, I think. He went missing from a beach on holiday."

The woman scribbled something down and I wished I'd kept my mouth shut. More people were piling into the Rectory now. I don't think it had ever been so busy.

"We'll need to look into that. And we're going to be conducting door-to-door enquiries with all your neighbours," she added.

"You're not gonna try and pin this on Old Nina, are you?"

She frowned. "We're just after the truth, Jake. Now, if you'll excuse me, I need to get on. If there's anything else you want to tell us, then do give me a call." She took a card from her pocket and passed it to me, before hurrying off into a waiting car.

Mum was downstairs sitting in the lounge, staring at the blank TV. She looked odd, just looking at the screen like that.

I picked up the remote and turned it on. I scrolled through the channels. "What do you want to watch, Mum? A film? The news? Something about cooking?" Mum continued to stare ahead as if she didn't care. I stopped on the weather forecast.

I turned and looked at her. It was like I wasn't there. Why couldn't she start acting like my mum again? Maybe some news would shock her back to her old self?

"Did you hear the police knock earlier, Mum? Old Nina has been arrested. A skeleton has been found in her garden. Wilson dug it up! I was there. Me!"

Mum looked up at me then, but her eyes were blank. "Oh dear," she said.

"Is that all you can say? Everyone is over at Matthew's house talking about it. You should be there too, you know."

Mum shook her head. "No. I can't do that," she said.

"Leo messaged me. He said he's been texting you but you haven't been answering." I blurted it out before I had really thought about it.

There was terror on Mum's face as she sat upright. "You haven't told him anything, have you?" she asked. "Please tell me you haven't."

I swallowed. "I said you were like you were before but worse. You've got to tell someone, Mum! You've got to go to the doctor."

Mum's face fell and she kept rubbing the top of her hands over and over and shaking her head.

"You shouldn't have done that, Jake. You can't tell anyone. I–I don't know what will happen to you if … if I can't look after you, Jake. You won't say any more, will you? Not to Leo or Auntie Wendy or any of the neighbours?"

I wished my brother was here. He would know what to do. But he was on the other side of the world. And there wasn't anyone else. Maybe she was right. Maybe not telling anyone was the best thing to do and then she could just get better in her own time? She'd promised she would ring the doctor tomorrow, hadn't she?

"I won't say anything," I muttered.

She dropped her head against the sofa for a

moment and stared back at the television screen. There was an advert on for a holiday at a sandy beach with palm trees and a turquoise-blue sea.

"I think I'll go back to bed," she said. She clutched her dressing gown to her chest and stood up, wobbling slightly, then made her way to the stairs.

I picked up the remote to turn the TV off when a presenter in a blue spotty shirt began to read the local news headlines.

"The remains of an adult male have been discovered in a garden in Chestnut Close. At the moment the cause of death has not been confirmed, nor the identification of the deceased. The police have issued a statement saying that a woman living at the address has been arrested and is currently being questioned."

I pulled the curtain back a fraction and looked over at the Rectory. The police officer had kept her promise, at least. The orange lamp in the window was lit once more.

I had a bad night. To start with I couldn't get to sleep. I kept thinking about Mum and the skull and what was going to happen to Old Nina, and then, when I eventually drifted off, I had a nightmare. I dreamed I was in the kitchen, feeding Wilson, when

I saw four skeletons standing motionless in our back garden. I was paralysed with fear and just stood there, staring at them from the window. Mum wandered down from her bedroom, opened the back door and went straight out on to the lawn in her bare feet and dressing gown. She began to dance and then, ever so slowly, the skeletons began to move too, their bones rattling and clanking.

"Come and dance, Jake!" Mum called to me, a wide grin on her face. "It's fun!"

I went to the kitchen door and slammed it shut, waking up with a jolt.

I drifted in and out of sleep after that, and when my alarm went off my heart was still racing and I felt like I'd been awake all night.

I groaned as I pushed myself up on my pillows. I wondered how Nina was. She must have had to sleep in a police cell. I hoped she hadn't been cold and that they'd looked after her, even if they did think she was a criminal.

Beside my alarm clock was the silver ring I'd found in Nina's garden. I picked it up and looked again at the faint letters round the inside. I'd completely forgotten about this. Could it have something to do with the body? Maybe I should pass it on to the police. That officer had given me her card yesterday so I could call her, I guess. But would that cause more problems for Nina? I decided to take it to school and see what Matthew and Melody thought when I showed them.

I got in the shower, flinching as the water hit my sore skin. Even though it made my stomach churn, I decided that if Mum still hadn't done it, I would call the doctor after school. She needed help and *I* needed my prescription. I got dressed, wearing the same dirty shirt from the past few days, then checked on Mum. She was asleep. I had some toast, then made Mum a cup of coffee and a bowl of cornflakes and put them on her bedside table.

Our doorbell went and I hurried downstairs, wondering if it was some news about the skeleton, but it was Melody. She was holding three large Tupperware tubs in her arms.

"Hi, Jake! Mum said you can have these for your dinner," she said, thrusting them towards me.

They were freezing and appeared to contain various shades of brown sludge.

"Thanks," I said. They were sticking to my hands, so I hurried to the kitchen to put them down. Melody followed, making a fuss of Wilson, who was jumping up at her legs.

"Mum said if you want one tonight, just leave it out to defrost, then blast it in the microwave. Oh, the police knocked at ours last night! They asked Mum if she'd noticed anything suspicious going on at the Rectory. They've spoken to everyone, I think."

"Any news on Nina?" I asked.

Melody shook her head. "Nothing. Mum thinks they can keep her for twenty-four hours and then they need to get an extension to hold her if they aren't going to charge her. Mum asked the police officer if they would feed Pepper while she's not there and he agreed."

Melody looked around the kitchen then. It was such a mess. Plates, mugs and saucepans were piled high in the sink and the bin was still overflowing. She stared at everything, blinking, then looked up at me.

"Jake? Is everything all right?"

I picked up a filthy tea towel and crammed it into the already full washing machine, then put some dirty cups and bowls closer to the sink.

"Yes? Why wouldn't it be?" I snapped.

Melody stared at the pink shirts hanging out on the washing line. I still hadn't brought them in.

"I'm just behind with stuff," I said quickly. "I'll wash up later, if Mum doesn't get to it first. She said she's not feeling so bad today."

Melody nodded. "Oh, that's good," she said, looking a little relieved.

"Come on, we'd better go now," I said, practically pushing her out of our house.

Out on the close, things were busy. The police tape was still draped across the front of the gate of the Rectory and a uniformed officer stood on the step. There was a van and a police car parked outside and the white tent was still up in the back garden.

We stood at the end of Matthew's driveway, and I looked at the top window of his house and saw his silhouette moving from left to right. When he was at his worst with his OCD he used to spend a lot of time in that room, watching the world from the window. He was there so much that Mr Charles's granddaughter, Casey, nicknamed him the Goldfish Boy, thinking he looked like a goldfish behind glass in a fish tank. He hated that. And I was quite mean to him too, which I'm not proud about.

A few moments later, the front door opened and Matthew came out, hurrying towards us.

"All right?" he said.

I fondled the ring in my pocket, as we began to walk.

"I meant to tell you. I found something else in

Nina's garden. A couple of weeks ago," I said. I stopped walking and took the ring out.

"Ooh. Can I have a look?" said Melody. She took the ring and inspected it closely.

"I spotted it in the grass when I was mowing her lawn. Nina didn't have a clue where it had come from and she said I could keep it. I don't think it's valuable or anything. It looks like metal or tin. Or it could be silver maybe," I said.

Melody held the ring close to her eye and squinted at it. "It's hallmarked, I think. And there are some letters on there, too." She twirled it round in her fingers, looking at the pattern on the outside.

"It looks like a wedding ring," said Matthew. "It's that kind of shape anyway. You should probably hand it over to the police, Jake. It might belong to the victim. Or the murderer!"

Melody handed the ring back to me, a big grin on her face. "Let's not rush into telling the police just yet," she said. "I think we could do a bit of detective work ourselves first, don't you?"

Chapter 10

A Closer Inspection

At breaktime I hurried to find Matthew and Melody. They were hanging around in our usual spot near the snack shop.

"Do you have that ring, Jake?" said Matthew.

"Yep," I said, patting my trouser pocket.

"Good. Come on, we're going to see Mr Turner," said Melody.

Mr Turner teaches science and is one of my favourite teachers. For one thing, he never seems to lose his temper and when someone plays up in class he just stops and stares at whoever it is and says something funny like: "Have you finished or are you going for the world record for being annoying?" That usually makes whoever it is laugh and, bam, we're back to learning about friction or something like that. He also likes playing music in his room when he isn't teaching, and we could hear a reggae track as we approached his door. Through the window we saw him sitting at his desk with a large mug of coffee, his head nodding left and right to the music.

Melody knocked and went in.

"Mr Turner. Can we have some help, please?" she said.

Matthew and I sloped in behind her.

"Miss Bird! How can I help you?" said Mr Turner, turning the volume down on the little cube speaker on his desk.

"Can we borrow a magnifying glass? We're trying to read something on an old silver ring that Jake found."

I took the ring out of my pocket.

Mr Turner frowned and took it from me. He brushed his thumb round the band, looking at the intricate pattern on the outside. "Where did you get this from?" he asked.

"I found it in my neighbour's garden," I told him. "She said I could keep it. I think it might be old."

Mr Turner peered closely at the ring. "The dirt

probably makes it appear older than it is." He squinted at the inside. "There are hallmarks on here. Wait there a minute."

He got up and went to a room at the back where the lab equipment was kept. He came out with a little tear-shaped object that he flipped open. It was a lens of some sort, and reminded me a little of the miniscope thing that Melody had bought for me years ago.

He held it and the ring up to his eye. Then he passed them to me. "Take a look, Jake. What can you see?"

It was hard to see anything to start with. It was just blurry – until I got the distance right between the ring and the lens, and then some numbers came into view.

"Erm. I can see a tent shape. And" – I moved the ring away a little and it came into focus – "there's a number inside it. It says nine, five, zero."

"Yes!" said Mr Turner, looking quite excited. He ran his hands through his black hair, tucking it behind his ears. "And do you know what 'nine, five, zero' in a little tent means?"

"Is it a hallmark for silver?" asked Matthew.

"No. It's platinum! One of the most precious metals out there."

"Oh, wow," I said.

"There is something else engraved on there too, isn't there?" said Melody. "Can I have a try?"

She took the ring and lens. "There's a 'P' and a 'K', I think," she said. She stuck her tongue between her teeth as she concentrated. "Yes. It's definitely a 'P' and a 'K' and a '21' … a '7' … and then a '79'." She put her hands down. "Twenty-first of July 1979."

"It sounds like a wedding date to me," said Mr Turner. "That looks like a classic wedding band and the couple must have had it engraved on the inside, marking the day of their marriage. There might be a maker's mark too? Can you see anything else?"

Melody offered it to Matthew, but he shook his head, so I took it back. I could see the letters and date clearly now. And just after the date there was another kind of stamp.

"I can see two Es and a small star," I said.

"Two Es? Ah, probably a jeweller's mark. There's a jeweller on the high street called Evangeline Ernest," said Mr Turner. "She's been there for years, so it might be one she made."

"Oh, I know that shop! Dad bought Mum some earrings for Christmas there once," said Matthew.

I put the ring back into my pocket and gave Mr Turner the lens. "Thank you, sir," I said.

"No problem at all," said Mr Turner, sitting back in his chair. "You're trying to get it back to its rightful owner, are you?"

"Something like that," I mumbled. I didn't think it sounded good that we were actually trying to identify a dead body, or possibly a murderer.

"I'm sure the jeweller's will have records of who ordered the ring. They'll probably be able to tell you straight away who it belonged to," said Mr Turner.

I could sense Melody fidgeting. She was getting excited.

"Great! Thanks, sir," she said.

The bell went for the end of break and we headed out of the classroom.

"Shall we pay Evangeline Ernest a visit on the way home, then?" said Matthew.

I nodded. "Yes, let's do it."

I felt a fizzle of excitement in my tummy. It was nice to have something else to think about apart from Mum or Old Nina or the mess in our kitchen that I'd have to tackle at some point. I also liked spending even more time with Matthew and Melody, who had become like family to me, even if they didn't realize it.

Chapter 11

Evangeline Ernest

It took forever for the final bell of the school day to ring, but eventually it rang out through the corridors and I hurried from my last lesson to the school gates. I stepped to one side to try and avoid the mass of bodies flowing to the exit. A group of younger kids were messing around, swinging their bags at each other and laughing when they hit each other's legs, making them buckle. The teacher on duty yelled at them to stop.

Melody arrived, giving me a playful thump on my shoulder. "Ready to go?" she said with a big smile.

Matthew was behind her. "I can't be ages, you two," he said. "I've got to go somewhere."

Again? I noticed he had a second bag over his shoulder – a small black drawstring bag that was a bit like the one I used to carry my EpiPen in when I wasn't in school. I was pretty sure he didn't have PE today, so what was that for? Melody clocked it too and she shrugged at me.

Evangeline Ernest Jewellers was one of those shops on the high street that I must have walked past hundreds of times and never noticed. The windows were dimly lit and the sign above the door was black with the shop name in gold lettering.

We peered in at the trays of necklaces, earrings and rings all twinkling in the sunlight.

"Shall we go in?" said Matthew, checking his watch. He was clearly thinking about where else he needed to be.

Melody pushed the door and a little bell tinkled above us. A woman came from the back of the shop. She was wearing a lemon-coloured dress and grey cardigan and had greying hair that was scooped up with a big clip at the back of her head. She rested her hands on a glass counter.

"Can I help you?" she asked, frowning. I doubted she had many schoolchildren visiting her shop.

I didn't really want to do the talking and I looked at Matthew, who didn't say anything either. Melody blinked at me. Waiting for me to say something as it was my ring, I guess.

"Um. I've got this ring," I said. "And, um, I wanted to find out who owned it so we can, um, get it back to them."

I cringed. I wasn't as good at talking as Melody, but the woman seemed friendly and gave me a smile.

"I see. That's kind of you. May I take a look?"

I got the ring out of my pocket and put it on the counter.

"It's got a maker's mark on it. EE," said Melody.

"And we thought it was probably made here," said Matthew. "Or our teacher did, anyway."

The woman nodded as she took out a little eyeglass like Mr Turner had used. "Yes, that's one of ours, for sure. But it's an old one. 1979." She put the ring down. "We do have some records dating back to then. My mother might remember something about it. I'll just get her." She disappeared through a door and came back with a woman who looked like an older, shorter version of her. The older woman was also wearing a grey cardigan but over a navy dress, with white hair clipped back.

"Hello. I hear one of you has found one of my rings. I'm Evangeline," she said, looking at each of us in turn.

"I did," I said, pushing the ring forward.

Evangeline took the lens and held up the ring, studying it closely. When she put the lens down, she wasn't smiling any more.

"Rose, darling, could you get the accounts book for May 1979, please?" she said. "I just want to check something."

Rose went back through the door and Evangeline sat down on a stool beside the till. She looked shaken.

"Do you know who the owner was?" said Matthew.

"I ... I think ... I think I do," said Evangeline.

Rose returned with an old leather-bound book that she placed on the glass counter, opening it up.

"Darling, could you look towards the end of the month at the orders for engraving? There will be a name in there and a description of the work," said Evangeline.

I watched her. She was breathing fast and had her clenched hand pressed against her mouth.

Rose flicked through the book. "OK, this is for the tenth of May and then the seventeenth of May..."

"Later than that. The twenty-something, I think," said Evangeline.

"This is amazing!" said Melody. "This was years ago, but you can still remember your customers. How incredible!"

But I thought there was something about Evangeline's reaction that was worrying.

"Something happened back then, didn't it?" I asked. "That's why you remember."

Evangeline looked up at me and I thought I could see something in her eyes. Fear.

"What am I looking for, Mum?" said Rose.

Evangeline cleared her throat. "Look for an order for a Mr Johnson," said Evangeline. "A Mr Paul Johnson."

Rose ran a finger down the large book and then stopped. "Ah, here we are. An order for an etched platinum wedding ring with an engraving of the initials 'P' and 'K' and the date 21.7.79. That must be the one," she said, reading the page and smiling. Then her face dropped. "Oh. He never paid," she said.

She turned the book round so that we could see.

"Back then Mum used to write a date in this box when the order had been fulfilled," she said, tapping on a square. In the box in bright red pen 'UNPAID' was written in large letters.

"He was full of charm, that one," said Evangeline slowly. "Told me an elaborate story about how he was going to surprise his fiancée with the inscription on his ring on their wedding day and how he planned to come back and buy her a diamond necklace. He seemed so genuine. But he wasn't. He was a very bad man." She took a deep breath and shuddered as she let it out.

There was a glass of water by the till and Evangeline took a sip and then placed it back down.

"He came in to see the ring and the inscription to make sure he was happy with it. I never insist on anyone paying unless they're happy," she said. "He tried it on and put it back in the little box, saying he needed to go to the bank to withdraw the cash."

Evangeline took another sip of water. "He didn't come back for hours. I thought that was very strange, so I called the number he'd given me, but the phone had been disconnected. When I checked the ring box, it had gone. He had stolen the ring from right under my nose."

"That must have been horrible," I said.

She nodded. "And to make it worse, we had a burglary that week and everything was taken – all the jewellery, money from the safe, everything. Rose was just a young child and I was a single mother. It was not an easy time."

"Did the police ever catch who burgled you? Or that man, Mr Johnson, for taking the ring?" said Matthew.

Evangeline shook her head. "No. But I think they are the same person. Paul Johnson stole the ring and he came back three days later and burgled my shop while Rose and I were asleep in the flat upstairs."

"How do you know it was him who burgled you?" asked Melody.

Evangeline sighed. "I don't have any proof, just my intuition. When he was here he was really interested in the jewelled necklaces and the bangles, asking me questions about prices and what precious metals I'd used. I thought he was just being friendly, but after the robbery I became convinced he was staking out the shop before he struck. But, like I say, I can't prove anything." She took a tissue out of her pocket and pressed it to her lips.

Rose put her hand on her mum's arm. "Why don't you go and sit down and I'll come and make us a nice cup of tea in a minute, OK, Mum?"

Evangeline nodded. "It was lovely to meet you," she said to us, before heading back through the door.

"Sorry we've upset your mum," said Melody. "We had no idea the ring belonged to such a bad person."

"You weren't to know," said Rose, closing the accounts book. "But I wouldn't bother trying to trace him if I were you. It sounds to me like he is best avoided."

"You should have the ring back if it's stolen property," I said, holding it up. Rose looked at the ring, then shook her head. "No. You keep it. Sell it for charity or something. I don't think we want it back. Not with all those bad memories."

We thanked Rose and left the shop, the bell tinkling on our way out.

"Wowzers," said Melody. "What do we think? Is Paul Johnson the murderer?"

"I don't know. But if he was, why did he bury a body in Old Nina's back garden?" I said.

Matthew took his phone out of his blazer.

"So what now? We give the ring to the police, I guess?" I said. "I mean, we can't withhold possible evidence, can we?"

Matthew looked up from his phone and stopped walking.

"There's more news," he said. "Look at this."

He turned his phone and on the screen were the headlines for a local news story:

BODY IN GARDEN NAMED AS LOCAL BUSINESSMAN PRESTON JAMES

Matthew turned the phone back and read. "It says here he went missing in 1999, aged fifty. Oh, and it says that Nina has been released on bail. She's out!"

He looked up. I felt relieved but I knew that being on bail meant she wasn't in the clear yet. It meant they were still doing their investigations into what happened.

There was a beep and Melody took her phone out next.

"It's from Mum! She said that Nina is staying with us for a while," said Melody. "I guess she's not allowed to go home maybe?"

We started walking again, a little more quickly this time.

"So how did Preston James end up buried in Old Nina's garden?" said Matthew.

"And more importantly, who killed him?" I said.

Chapter 12

A Secret Chat

Matthew went in a different direction when we got to the main traffic lights in town saying he had to be somewhere, and Melody and I headed home. We were so into our investigations that we didn't think to talk about what Matthew might be up to.

"If we can find out more about Preston James, we might be able work out what he was doing at Nina's," said Melody.

"And then we can rule out her having anything to do with him ending up dead in her garden," I said.

"Hmmm. Maybe," said Melody.

Melody didn't sound convinced, but I still

wanted to believe that there was no way Nina had anything to do with that dead body. The thought of her going to jail was unthinkable and I knew deep in my bones that she wasn't a murderer. I'd enjoyed spending time with her in the Rectory. It was probably selfish of me, but I didn't want to lose her like I was losing Mum.

When we got to the close there was a blue car on Melody's drive.

"Oh, there's Dad already," said Melody. "I'm going to his for dinner. I promised Maisie I'd read her a bedtime story."

Melody had only recently started seeing her dad again. He'd moved out a few years ago and she had found it really hard and hadn't see him for a while, so it was nice that she'd made up with him. She also adored Maisie, her little half-sister. I'd never known my dad, which was a shame, because I could really do with a dad right now. Or really just *anyone else* to be in charge so that I didn't have to look after Mum all on my own.

"See you tomorrow, Jake," Melody said. Then she hurried over to the car. Her dark, plaited hair swinging down her back as she went.

When I got home I saw Mum's phone on the

kitchen counter. Her manager had texted, asking when she was going to return to work. She hadn't answered, so I replied, pretending to be her. I said,

> SUE: Flu better. Now got a chest infection. Can't come back yet.

I remembered Auntie Wendy had once been ill for weeks with a chest infection so I thought that would give her some more time. But the manager replied straight away, saying that they'd need a certificate from her doctor or she wouldn't get any sick pay.

I raced upstairs to tell Mum.

"Mum? Are you awake?"

I listened to her breathing and saw the duvet gently rising and falling in the gloomy light.

"Mum? You did call the doctor, didn't you?"

She didn't answer.

"You promised you'd call them. Remember? You need to see them and get a certificate or something or you won't get sick pay."

There was movement and her head slowly appeared. She stared up at the ceiling.

"I just can't face it, Jake. Not today." Her head turned away and I thundered downstairs. How could she let me down like this? This had gone on for too long. If Mum was too poorly or tired or overwhelmed or whatever it was to call the doctor, I'd just have to do it for her. I would ask for my eczema cream at the same time. I searched for the number online using my phone and pressed call, my stomach churning nervously as it rang. I didn't like doing this one little bit. It felt too grown-up and I was worried that I might say something silly, or they might not be able to help, but I spoke to a nice woman who said that my cream would be ready in the pharmacy in a couple of days, but she couldn't get an appointment for Mum until next week. At least it was something. When I hung up I realized I hadn't asked about the certificate Mum's boss mentioned, but hoped that Mum would sort that out when she was seen.

That evening I heated up some of the food that Melody had dropped off earlier. It was steaming hot after its spin in the microwave and looked pretty disgusting, but I tried a spoonful and it tasted amazing. While I was eating, my phone pinged. It was a message from Matthew to me and Melody.

MATTHEW: I've been thinking. Where did you find the ring, Jake? Was it near where the skeleton was found?

JAKE: No. It was on the grass near the house.

MATTHEW: Hmmm. So maybe there was a fight between Paul Johnson and Preston James and it fell off.

Melody was typing.

MELODY: Mum said she asked Nina if she'd heard of Preston James and she said no and that the police had showed her his photo and she didn't recognize him. I think she's lying!

JAKE: Of course she doesn't know him!

MATTHEW: Maybe the murderer killed Preston somewhere else and just buried him in Nina's garden?

JAKE: YES! That sounds more likely.

MELODY: Hmmm. We'll see. Mum is taking her to the police station in the morning. She has to report there as part of her bail conditions.

Poor Nina.

MELODY: Let's talk tomorrow. I've got to read "We're Going on a Bear Hunt" for the *tenth* time ☺

It was getting late and I still hadn't taken Wilson out, so I got his lead and clipped it on to his collar. My phone pinged again. This time it was Leo.

LEO: How's things? Has Mum seen the doctor yet?

I stood in the hallway, thinking what I should say. Mum's reaction when she'd found out I'd told Leo she was unwell had worried me. She didn't even know I'd made her a doctor's appointment yet. How would she react to that?

JAKE: Not yet. But she's going next week.

LEO: Great! Well done, Jakey.

It was funny how my big brother was suddenly nice to me now he was on the other side of the world. Maybe he was realizing I wasn't so bad after all. I guess being away from your family can do that.

Wilson began to whine.

"Come on. Let's go," I said with a sigh.

I walked down our driveway and turned into the alleyway beside the Rectory. I could hear the police and investigation team mumbling in the back garden. I shuddered when I thought about what I'd found at the end of that stick. There was a police officer at the back of her garden too, and she gave me a nod as I passed.

I did a loop round the middle of the graveyard, which wasn't very long, but I hoped Wilson wouldn't mind. I liked walking in the graveyard with Melody and Matthew, but I found it a bit creepy on my own, and I jumped when a bright orange leaf fluttered down beside me. I hurried past the stone angels, not looking at them in case they moved, and back towards the alleyway.

When I came out on to the close I noticed the door of Melody's house opening. I thought it was going to be Claudia, as Melody was at her dad's, but it was Old

Nina. I gave her a wave and she beckoned me over. I glanced towards the police officer standing on her step just staring down at nothing. I crossed the road and Wilson wagged his tail, happy for his walk to be carrying on.

"Oh, Jake. What a terrible, terrible time," Old Nina said. Her white hair, which was usually neatly curled and pinned at the sides, was loose and wispy, and she was wearing a baggy grey dress and some thick blue socks. She looked tired and very frail.

"Are you all right, Nina?"

She ignored my question and kept checking over my shoulder towards the police officer and then down the road. She reached out her arm and her cold hand rested on top of mine.

"I need you to do something for me, Jake. But you mustn't tell anyone. Do you promise?"

I stared at her as she chewed on the inside of her cheek. I thought she looked close to tears.

"Um. What is it?"

She looked down the road again, then back to me.

Her cold hand gripped mine tightly. She shook it a little. "I need you to—" There was the sound of a car turning into the road. Nina straightened, a weak smile on her face. She let go of my hand.

"What is it?" I asked. "What do you need me to do?"

But Nina did a tiny shake of her head as Claudia's car swung on to the driveway. She clearly didn't want anyone else to hear what she was about to ask me.

"Hi, Nina. Everything OK?" said Claudia, closing her car door with a bang. She looked between the two of us, a quizzical expression on her face.

I kept my eyes on Nina but she was silent.

"Jake?" said Claudia.

"Oh, I, erm, I was just walking Wilson and thought I'd see how things are," I said. I felt my cheeks blush at the fib.

"That's kind of you," said Claudia. "Are you OK, Nina? Do you want a cup of tea or anything to eat?"

"No, dear. I'm fine," said Nina. "I'm going to go for a sit-down." Her forehead was furrowed as she gave me a final look and then they both went inside.

I crossed back to my house. I didn't want to admit it but this didn't feel right. What was it that Nina was about to ask me that she couldn't say in front of Claudia?

Was it something to do with Preston James? Surely Old Nina wasn't involved in some way.

Was she?

Chapter 13

Into The Cellar

The next day I'd forgotten all about Nina's strange behaviour. I'd also become used to seeing the police as they went in and out of the Rectory. But then we came home from school, and everyone had gone. The Rectory was no longer draped in police tape like some oddly wrapped birthday present. There were no strange cars parked in every available space, and the white tent that had stood in the back garden had vanished. It was as if none of it had ever happened.

We stood by the NOW LET sign outside number one.

"Isn't it quiet?" said Matthew as he looked around at our empty road.

"It's eerie," said Melody.

The door to number three opened and Claudia hurried out, pulling a thick knitted green cardigan round herself.

"Hello, Melody, love," she said as she joined us. "Good news. The police have lifted Nina's bail and she can go home, but she's asked if she can stay with us a while longer. Is that OK with you? She's not up to being on her own just yet"

Melody nodded. "Yes, of course, Mum."

Claudia smiled. "Thank you," she said. "Apparently the police are looking at other leads now."

"That's great news!" I said, my heart lifting. I *knew* she was innocent.

Claudia turned to me. "How's your mum, Jake? I thought she'd be up and about by now, but I haven't seen her." She casually put an arm through Melody's.

"Oh, she's got, um, a chest infection," I said, doing a nervous cough myself.

"That's rotten! Poor Sue. Give her my love, won't you?"

"I will," I said.

We all headed home and I checked on Mum,

getting her a glass of water, and then I attempted to do a bit of washing-up. I'd only managed to get through two cereal bowls when our doorbell rang.

Wilson beat me there and was wiggling madly on the doormat. It was Old Nina.

"Oh, hello," I said.

"Hello, Jake," she said quietly. "Claudia has some food for you and your mum, and I offered to bring it over so I could get a bit of fresh air. But I also wanted a word with you if I'm honest."

She held out a large paper bag and I could see inside there were more tubs of home-made meals, milk, bananas and a loaf of bread. What a relief!

"Great! Thank you," I said, taking the bag.

I stood there, waiting. As usual it was hard to tell if Nina had finished talking or if she was about to say something else.

"Um, I didn't get the chance to ask you yesterday because Claudia turned up and … I couldn't ask in front of her. But … but there's something I wanted you to do for me."

"Oh. Right," I said.

Her eyes flicked to the ground. "I want you to go in my house and get something for me. I would do it but I don't think I can manage it," she said. She did look more frail than usual. I think a strong gust of wind could have blown her over.

"OK," I said.

She wrung her hands together, her eyes still lowered. "It might be nothing, but I'm worried the police will find it and want to take me into that dreadful place again." Her pale blue eyes darted up to mine.

"What is it you need me to get?" I asked.

"I need you to go down to my cellar."

My mouth dropped open. She wanted me to go in her *cellar*?

Nina continued. "The door is in the corner of the kitchen. It looks like a cupboard but it's not. Take a torch and go down the steps and when you get to the bottom walk forward. At the end, on the right-hand side, there's a little alcove."

She looked so scared. But this wasn't making any sense. "I thought everything was OK now? Claudia said the police are looking at other leads."

Nina nodded, dropping her head again. "They are. But, you see, there's something I didn't tell them. And if they discover this, then … then I might be in trouble."

A car pulled on to next door's driveway and Kyle climbed out.

Nina stepped closer towards me and began to whisper, "There's a heavy trunk in front of the alcove. I don't think the police realized there was a space behind it. If they did … well, I probably wouldn't still be here."

She looked over at Kyle's car and turned her head slightly. "You need to get what's behind the trunk and hide it. Can you do that? The key to the front door is under the pot with the pink flowers."

Kyle was getting his bassoon case out of the car boot. I could sense him looking over at us.

"But what is it, Nina? What's in the alcove?" I whispered back.

She pulled her cardigan tight round her, and Kyle called over.

"Hello, Nina. Lovely to see you out and about. How are you doing?" He approached the fence that divided our driveways.

"Not too bad, thank you," said Nina. And then she gave me one more imploring look, before hurrying down our driveway and across the road. I nodded at Kyle, then closed the door and took a deep breath. Did that really just happen? What was it she wanted me to hide? I took my phone and typed a message to Matthew and Melody. I was worried about what might be hidden in a dark corner of her cellar, but there was no way I would let Nina down. There was also no way I was going to venture into the dark corners of her house on my own.

JAKE: OLD NINA HAS ASKED ME TO DO SOMETHING!

I had to wait a bit until someone answered. I guessed they were both catching up with their families, chatting about their days.
Matthew messaged first.

MATTHEW: To do what?

MELODY: Yes, Jake! What does she want you to do?

I felt guilty betraying Old Nina's secret. But going into the Rectory in the daytime was creepy enough, let alone at night *and* in the cellar.

JAKE: Meet me by the Rectory at 11 p.m. And bring a torch! I'll explain everything then. And don't tell your parents!

That evening I heated some of Claudia's food. I took some up for Mum, but she was asleep again. I saw she'd eaten the toast I'd left her that morning, though, so at least that was something.

I spent the rest of the evening gaming and thinking about cleaning up and not actually doing it, and then it was time.

Wilson followed me to the front door and watched me with his head on one side as I put on my jacket and zipped it up. I swung my small sports kit bag containing my EpiPen on to my back.

Wilson whined and I stroked his head.

"I won't be long," I whispered. He settled down by the foot of the stairs and rested his head between his paws.

I went out and closed the door as silently as I could.

Melody and Matthew were already standing at the end of the alleyway. Melody had the same torch she'd brought to my birthday party in the tent – the massive one that nearly lit up the whole street.

She put it under her chin and pulled a face. "Oooh, I'm a dancing skeleton!" she said, giggling and moving her arms about.

"It wasn't funny then, and it's not funny now," I

whispered. "Come on, before anyone sees us. We're going into the Rectory."

"What?" said Matthew. "But what about the murder? We can't go in there!"

"Matthew is right. We probably shouldn't."

I ignored them both and went to the front step of Old Nina's house. I shifted the pot of flowers out of the way and found a small gold key. I quickly fitted it into the lock and opened it.

"Jake! What are you doing?" said Matthew in a hushed voice.

I stepped into the house and, before I could close the door, Matthew and Melody hurried up the path and bundled in beside me. The door slowly closed behind us with a long creak.

Matthew shuddered and checked all around using the torch on his phone. There was a dull glow coming from the lamp in Nina's lounge, but it was still very dark. "Crikey. Can we put a light on at least? This place is so creepy."

"Of course we can't! Someone will call the police," said Melody. "What are we doing in here, Jake? You'd better hurry up and explain yourself."

"Nina said there's something hidden in the house that I need to find and then I've got to hide it for her."

"What?!" said Matthew loudly.

"Shhhh!!" said Melody.

"And you agreed to this?" said Matthew in a whisper.

"She's worried about something!" I said. "And I want to help."

"What is it you need to get?" said Melody.

"I–I don't know," I said.

"Oh, that's just great," said Matthew. "I'm sorry, Jake, but this is wrong. What if it's the murder weapon?"

"Of course it's not a weapon. This is Old Nina, remember? The police aren't even investigating her any more. Melody's mum said they've got other leads."

"So why all the secrecy?" said Melody.

I shrugged. "I don't know."

"This is sounding well dodgy," said Matthew, shaking his head.

"Listen. I don't know what I'm looking for, exactly. But I do know where it's hidden," I said. I didn't want my friends to give up on me.

"Go on. Where is it, then?" said Melody. "We can just grab it and go."

I swallowed. "Well, that's the thing. She said it's in the cellar."

Matthew began to laugh. "That's me out. I'm going home." He went to open the front door, but Melody put her hand on it to stop him.

"Oh, come on, Matthew. We've come this far. You're not scared, are you?"

Matthew pulled a face. "Hang on. Let me think. I'm in the creepiest house in the whole town, it's night-time, my daft friends are intending to go down into the cellar in the pitch black and, oh yes, a skeleton was found in the garden less than a week ago! So, yes. I am scared, Melody."

Melody nodded. "Me too."

"Me three," I said.

We all took a deep breath.

"I'll go," said Melody.

I smiled at her. Her bravery amazed me sometimes. "We'll both go," I said. "And you can be the lookout, Matthew. That sound OK? You both did want to come, by the way."

"That was before I knew you were coming in here! This place is terrifying. Look at it!" said Matthew, pointing his torch around the hallway. The beam reflected on to the collection of picture frames on the wall and he paused on the image of Nina's lost son, Michael, smiling in a school photo. I shivered.

"I'm going to look around first," said Melody. And before we could stop her, she trotted upstairs.

"Melody! What are you doing?" I said. "You can't just go running around her house!"

"There might be evidence in here!" she called.

Matthew and I stood there staring at each other. And then Melody gave an urgent whisper.

"Come and see this!"

I followed Melody up the stairs. Every step creaked and Matthew was so close behind me he nearly tripped me up. On the landing were four closed doors and one that was half open. I could see the light from Melody's torch inside.

"You really shouldn't be up here. This is private and—"

I stopped talking as I stood in the doorway.

Melody was standing in the centre of a bedroom, sweeping her torch slowly around the room. The bed was made with a blue striped duvet and there was a small stuffed gorilla sitting on the pillow. On the bedside table was a small white lamp, a black old-fashioned digital watch and a book called *Animal Farm* with a bookmark poking out of the pages about halfway through. In the corner was a single white wardrobe and on one wall were a couple of film posters from the 1990s. On another wall were rows of certificates. I took a closer look with my torch and saw they were awards for swimming.

"This is his room, isn't it?" said Melody. "Michael's. Her son who died."

"She's left it exactly how it must have been when he was alive," said Matthew.

It was so sad, but it was also really, really creepy.

"Come on. Let's do what we came here for," I said quietly.

I turned round and the three of us thundered down the stairs.

I headed to the kitchen. The tall glasses Nina had used for her homemade lemonade were standing in the sink. That felt like ages ago now, the afternoon when I'd shifted the pieces of shed and found the skull. I shivered.

The clock on the wall ticked loudly and there was a humming noise coming from the fridge. In the corner was a narrow wooden door that looked like a cupboard, just as Nina had described. I went over and took hold of the handle.

Melody joined me.

"You don't have to, you know," I said. "I made the promise. Not you."

Melody took a deep breath. "I know. But you can go first," she said.

I braced myself, then turned the handle.

The door was stiff and I had to tug it a few times to get it to open. A cold breeze hit my face and there was a damp smell. In front of us was a concrete staircase that led down to pitch-black nothingness.

"Look, there's a light switch," said Melody, pointing her torch to the slimy brown wall beside us. "No one will see us down there. Try it!"

I put my hand against the brass toggle and clicked it downwards, but nothing happened.

"Come on," I said. "Let's go."

I stepped tentatively on to the stone stairs, pressing my hand against the cold wall as I went. Down below I could see cardboard boxes piled high. It looked like a storage place for Nina's old things. I got to the bottom and waited for Melody.

"WHAT'S IT LIKE DOWN THERE?" yelled Matthew, making us both jump.

"Sshhh, Matthew!!" said Melody. "Right, Jake. What are we looking for?"

"She said to go straight ahead and on the right there's a heavy trunk. We need to shift it to get something out of an alcove." I took a few steps and swept the light from my torch around. It lit up what appeared to be someone's head and shoulders and I let out a squeal.

"What was that?!" shrieked Melody. "Is there someone there?" She grabbed my arm as her torch lit up a corner. We both let out a sigh of relief when we saw what it was.

"ARE YOU OK? What's going on?" called Matthew.

"It's a tailor's dummy!" Melody called back. "We're all right."

My heart was pounding in my chest. I wanted to find whatever it was and get out of there as soon as possible.

"Look! There's the trunk," I said. "Help me move it, Melody."

In the corner was a wooden box with a lid and brass handles at each end. I took one handle and Melody took the other and we began to try and drag it.

"I wonder what's in this. It's so heavy!" said Melody, as she pulled.

"I don't know. But I'm not opening it to find out," I said. We moved it a centimetre at a time until there was enough space for me to squeeze behind it. At first I couldn't see anything, but then my light hit a slim brown suitcase that was tucked in the corner against the wall.

"That must be it. Keep your torch shining that way, Melody," I said. I got down on my hands and knees and crawled towards the case, reaching it with my fingertips. I eased it out until I could get a grip on the handle then reversed back out.

I stood up, holding the suitcase. It felt quite heavy and clearly had something inside.

"Shall we go?" I said, but Melody was already running up the stairs.

Back in the kitchen, I put the suitcase on the table and we crowded round it.

"A suitcase?" said Matthew. "What's in it?"

"I don't know," I said. There was a layer of dust on the case, and I brushed as much off as I could with my hand. "Nina asked me to hide it, not open it."

"Well, you can't hide it without finding out what's inside," said Melody. "You need to know what it is that's such a big secret."

"Yes. Open it and then you can decide if you need to hand it over to the police," said Matthew.

I wished I could open it without Matthew and Melody being there, but they were involved now. I just had to hope that it wasn't going to be anything that would make Old Nina look guilty.

I placed my thumbs against the locks on the side and pushed. They released with a click and I lifted the lid.

Chapter 14

Inside The Case

The first thing I noticed as the case opened was the faint smell of a musty aftershave. On the top were some men's shirts, neatly folded, in shades of light purple and blue. Under those were some socks, again neatly folded in half.

"It's someone's stuff," said Matthew. There was a green toiletry bag on one side that he took out and unzipped. Inside was a comb, soap, a sponge, tweezers, deodorant, a silver razor, some shaving cream and a small silver key.

"What do you think this opens?" I said, reaching for the key. It was too small to be for a door.

"No idea. But hang on to it for now," said Melody.

I took my sports kit bag off my back, the one that carried my EpiPen, and popped the key inside. We carried on unpacking. There were two pairs of suit trousers, a pair of grey silk pyjamas with the initials 'P. J.' embroidered on the collar, black pants, two white vests and a beige thin-knit jumper.

At the bottom, beneath the clothes, was a small leather wallet. Matthew opened it and took out a bank card. He read the name. "*Mr Piers Jackson*. Who is Piers Jackson?" he said, looking up at us.

"I don't know. Is there anything else in there?" I said.

Matthew checked through the rest of the wallet. "No. Just some old money."

I held out my hand and he passed me the wallet. It was made of soft brown leather and I stroked the embossed initials that were in one corner – *P. J.* Things were starting to tie up a little in my head.

"So the man who stole the ring and potentially robbed Evangeline Everest's shop was called Paul Johnson," I said. "The dead man in the garden was Preston James. And whoever owned this suitcase was called Piers Jackson." I picked up the silk pyjamas with the embroidered letters on the collar and held them beside the initialled wallet.

"It can't be a coincidence that these names are all 'P. J.'s, can it?" I said.

"I see what you mean," said Melody, taking the wallet and looking at it closely.

My heart began to thump loudly. This was getting exciting. "Don't you think it makes sense that these three men are, in fact, one person?" I said.

"You could be right there," said Matthew.

"And the fact the police have identified the body as Preston James must mean that that is his real name. And I bet this case belonged to him!" said Melody.

We were really piecing it together now!

But then Melody's face dropped. "And if this *is* his suitcase, then Nina must have known him, after all. Why did she lie to the police?"

"But she didn't, Melody," I snapped back. I pointed at the bank card. "She knew someone called Piers Jackson. So she hasn't lied, has she?"

"Well, why be all secretive about it then?" said Matthew. "Why ask you to hide it?"

"I don't know," I said. It was a puzzle. Why *was* Nina acting secretively about it? Was she trying to hide something else? I remembered the police officer who had given me her card on the day they arrested Nina. It would be easy to ring her. But how much trouble would that put Nina in? I didn't want to risk it.

"So … if Paul Johnson, Preston James and Piers Jackson *are* all the same person … how did a dead man's suitcase end up in her cellar?" said Melody. "Nina doesn't seem as innocent now as she was half an hour ago. We have to take this to the police."

"No! I know Nina. She isn't capable of hurting anyone. She must have her reasons for not telling the police. We can't just drop her in it when we don't know the facts," I said.

"It could be a victim's belongings, Jake," said Melody. "You can't keep quiet about it."

"It's my decision and it's going home with me," I said. "Old Nina is not a murderer."

"But it's not your property!" said Melody, grabbing one end of the case while I grabbed the other. "This could be used to solve Preston James's murder!" She tugged the case towards her.

"I'm not letting Nina down!" I said, tugging the case towards me.

"Don't be silly," said Matthew.

But we ignored him as we began to pull on the case like it was a tug of war game.

"Just give it up, Jake!" she shouted.

"It's not yours, Melody!" I yelled.

"I'll go to the police anyway!"

"Don't you dare do that behind my back!"

We now had the case at full stretch between the two of us, both of us refusing to let go.

"Just stop it! Both of you," said Matthew, shifting from foot to foot. "It's really late and I want to go to bed."

Melody let go and the case fell between us. As it landed there was a click and the lining inside seemed to pop open.

"Hang on. There's something under the bottom here," I said, crouching down. I felt around. "It's like a hidden compartment."

I put my fingernails under the edge of the base and lifted it, then jumped. "Urgh! There's something furry in there!" I said, pointing.

"What is it?" said Matthew, taking a few steps back.

Melody picked up a wooden spoon that was on the kitchen counter and used it to lift up the panel. She poked the spoon into the furry mass and lifted it up, reminding me of how I'd discovered the hideous skull.

"It's a wig!" she said. The dark hair dangled in

front of her, brown and glossy. "There's more in here too!" She used the spoon to move a rubbery-looking false nose, a selection of glasses and some make-up. These things wouldn't have looked out of place in the theatre or on a film set.

"Preston James must have used a disguise when he lived here," I said. "*That's* why Nina didn't recognize the photograph the police showed her."

Melody seemed deep in thought. "It does make sense. I guess he could have been in disguise when he visited Evangeline's shop as well."

Matthew had taken a few paces back. "Can we go? This is giving me the creeps," he said.

Melody dropped the wig back into the compartment and pushed the hidden panel down.

I piled everything back inside and then closed the case with a click. I looked at Melody who had her arms folded, glaring at me.

"We still need to pass this to the police," she said.

"Nina trusted me, Melody," I said. "I'm not going behind her back."

Melody huffed.

"Look. Why don't we see what we can find out about Preston James and then decide what to do?" said Matthew.

"OK," she said with a groan. "I guess it *is* intriguing. If Nina is innocent, how did a dead man's belongings end up here?"

"If we don't find any answers, then we hand it over," said Matthew. "Agreed?"

I picked up the handle of the case and swung it off the table.

"Agreed," I said. "Now, let's get out of here."

When I got home, I put the case down by the stairs and kicked off my trainers. I was exhausted and couldn't wait to get to bed. But then I heard a bang from the kitchen. I peered down the hallway and could see a light was on. Someone was in the house! Was it a burglar? Where was Wilson? I tiptoed down the hall. The kitchen door was wide open, and the wind was making it bang. I looked around for any signs that we'd been robbed, but the kitchen was in the mess that I'd left it. Then I spotted a figure standing in the middle of our lawn. It was Mum and she was staring up at the sky.

I hurried out.

"Mum? What are you doing?" She was wearing her thin dressing gown and her feet were bare. "You'll freeze!" Wilson was spinning around, clearly wondering what was going on. I slipped my jacket off and put it over her shoulders.

Mum kept her gaze fixed on the sky. "We're so small down here, aren't we?" she said.

I looked up. It was a clear, crisp night and there were tiny pinpricks of light twinkling in the sky.

"Come on, Mum. Let's get you inside."

We made our way indoors and she sat down while I locked up. When I looked back at her she was crying.

"I'm sorry, Jake. My thoughts keep running away from me and … I'm frightened."

She dropped her head and I put my arm round her. She was trembling from the cold.

"I called the doctor, Mum. I made you an appointment."

Mum looked up at me. "You did? Oh, Jake."

I thought she was going to be angry at me for going behind her back. But from the expression on her face I wondered if she was actually relieved.

"I couldn't get you seen until next week. They'll give you some tablets again like they did before, won't they? They'll make you feel better."

Mum cried quietly against my shoulder but she didn't say anything.

Wilson watched us from his basket, his eyes

drooping. We sat there for a few moments, and then I took her arm and guided her back to bed. She walked right past the suitcase without noticing it. After I'd settled her into bed, I ran down and got the case. In my bedroom I pulled my duvet out of the way, then slid the suitcase into the furthest, darkest corner underneath my bed. For now, that was where it was going to stay.

Chapter 15

The Visitor

I woke up and, for the first time in quite a while, I thought about not going to school. I had barely slept and I was so tired. And after last night I was worried about leaving Mum. What if she wandered out into the front garden and everyone saw her acting all weird? I lay there, weighing up whether to stay in bed all day like Mum, but then I thought it would make me feel worse just staring at my ceiling, and it was the last day before half-term, so I got up.

We weren't allowed to use our phones during school hours, so Matthew, Melody and I arranged to meet in the computer room at breaktime so we could investigate Preston James. We sat round one of the old PCs. Melody turned it on and we waited for it to spark into life and warm up.

"So far we know he married someone on the twenty-first of July 1979," said Matthew.

"And his wife's first name began with a 'K'," I said.

"And that he was likely a lying thief and used at least two other names with the same initials," said Melody.

Eventually the home page glowed in front of us, and Melody entered 'PRESTON JAMES' into the search engine. The computer whirred and a few lights on the base blinked.

"Blimey. This thing should be in a museum," said Matthew.

Eventually the search revealed its results. The first page was full of recent news articles about the discovery of the skeleton and it being identified as him. Melody clicked on a couple and they both pretty much said the same thing: that Preston James was a local businessman and that he had gone missing in the 1990s and that he had been a 'person of interest' to the police regarding some local thefts.

"So the police knew he was a criminal. Or

suspected he was, at least. Scroll down on the search results, Melody," I said.

"Hold on! Go back a bit," said Matthew. "There's something there." He pointed to an older local news article that had Preston James highlighted within the text.

Melody clicked on it. "It's about a cinema closing down on the high street years ago," she said.

I read some of the article out loud. "*'Unfortunately, we can't compete with the new multiplex that has been built at the edge of town,' said Diana Wilton, the manager of the cinema for the past twenty years. The owner of the cinema, local businessman Preston James, said it was a sad day but that there were currently no plans about what was going to become of the old building.*"

"What cinema? I've never seen one," said Melody.

"It's next to the Magpie pub where my dad's quiz team meets," said Matthew. Brian was a keen quizzer and his team Brian's Brains had won loads of trophies that were on display on a shelf in their lounge. Even though I had heard Sheila telling him many times that they should go in the loft.

The door to the computer room opened and one of

the IT support staff, Mr Gibson, was standing there with a bunch of cables in his hand. His jaw went up and down as he chewed gum.

"You lot have gotta shift. I've got to get these rebooted and virus checked before the Year Tens get here in approximately" – he checked his watch – "forty-six minutes."

"Oh. Can't we have just five more minutes, sir?" said Melody.

Mr Gibson sniffed. "Nope."

He pulled the keyboard we were using towards him and smacked a few of the keys and the screen went blank.

Matthew huffed and we picked up our bags and sloped out, heading to the playground.

"We should go to the cinema and see if we can find anything out about him there. There might be some old files or something?" I suggested.

"Yes!" Melody grinned. I knew she'd be up for something like this.

But Matthew wasn't so sure. "We can't just break into a private building!" he said. "It's trespassing."

"We're not going to do anything bad," I said. "We're just looking to see if we can find out anything else about Preston."

Matthew shook his head. "It'll be locked. We won't be able to get in."

"It's worth a look, at least," said Melody. "We don't have any other leads, do we?"

"You don't have to come, Matthew. I'll just go with Melody," I said.

But Matthew didn't like that one little bit. "I'm not missing out," he said. "I just want it known that I'm not happy about it."

Melody smirked at me. "Noted," she said.

The bell went for the end of break.

"Nearly half-term!" said Matthew, grinning.

"Can't wait," I said. I was looking forward to a break from school, and Mum had her appointment at the doctor's next week. As soon as she was on her medication again she'd be back to her old self.

My last lesson of the day was PE, which used to be my worst lesson, largely because I'd had a horrible teacher who made my life hell, but also because I hated having to get changed and everyone seeing my skin, which was worse than ever. But Mr Jenkins, the horrible teacher, had been replaced by Mr Proud, who was great. In PE we played badminton and I think I must have been quite good at it as, at the end, Mr Proud asked if I wanted to take part in an inter-school tournament in a few weeks' time. I said no. That wasn't what I did. Mr Proud just smiled and told me to think about it. But there was no way. I had had enough of people calling me names and pointing me out because of my skin, I didn't want to put myself up for something that could go horribly wrong.

I walked home with Matthew and Melody and we made our way along the high street.

"Is that the cinema over there?" I said.

Across the road was the Magpie pub and beside it was a large building with wide steps leading up to some glass doors. The glass doors had sheets of newspaper stuck to the inside so that you couldn't see in and there was lots of litter on the steps.

"Yep. That's it," said Matthew.

The old cinema was one of those buildings that had been there for ever so you somehow stopped really seeing it. There was an old film poster still in a frame beside the door with a SHOWING TONIGHT! banner stuck across the middle.

"I'm still not so sure about going in there," said Matthew, a worried expression on his face. "It kind of looks a bit ... grubby."

"It'll be fine," said Melody. "Let's come back tomorrow and investigate."

We turned into Chestnut Close and we were about to branch off to our houses when a dark car came crawling along the road. It came to a stop outside the Rectory.

"Who's that?" said Melody.

A man got out of the driver's side, then bent down, speaking to someone sitting in the front, before closing the door.

"Maybe it's the police?" said Matthew. "Maybe they've found more evidence and are back to rearrest her."

My stomach clenched for a second, but then I saw who was sitting in the passenger seat.

"I don't think they'd bring a kid to make an arrest, though, do you?" I said. "Look." It was a young boy. His head was dropped down as he looked at something in his hands.

The man turned around, looking at the close, then nodded at us. He looked to be in his forties or so with brown hair and a stubbly greying beard. He was wearing dark blue jeans and a black polo shirt. He went to the gate of the Rectory and walked up the path, then gave three loud raps with the heavy knocker.

As usual, Melody Bird couldn't help interfering.

Which was both annoying but also quite useful when you wanted to know what was going on.

"Can we help you?" said Melody, striding over to the Rectory.

Matthew and I followed her. The man frowned at us for a moment, then his face broke into a smile. "Hello! I'm looking for the woman who lives here. Nina Fennell? Do you know where she might be?"

"Who's asking?" I said, taking a step forward.

"Oh! Sorry. It must be suspicious having a stranger knocking on your neighbour's door. I'm guessing there's a tight-knit community in this street? You all look out for each other, I'm sure."

I looked the man up and down. "Who are you then?"

"I'm a relative of Nina's and, well, I want to make sure she's OK. I know she's had a terrible shock recently. I saw it on the news," said the man, pressing his lips together and shaking his head.

Matthew, Melody and I looked at each other. This didn't sound right. I'd lived in the close my whole life and I'd never known Nina to have one visitor, let alone a relative.

"Nina doesn't have any family," I said.

The man's forehead creased and he rubbed it with his fingers.

"I'm sorry, I know you're trying to protect your neighbour, but there's no need. I'm telling the truth. Nina Fennell *does* have family. Now can you tell me where she is, please?"

I folded my arms. There was no way I would let on where Nina was staying.

But then Matthew blurted out, "Nina isn't even living here right now. But if you were her family, you'd know that, wouldn't you?"

The man looked upset. There was the sound of a door opening behind us. He looked over our shoulders and we all turned round. Standing on the step of number three and wearing a navy skirt and a white blouse was Old Nina. She had probably seen there was someone outside her home and had come out to find out what was going on.

The man blinked as he watched her, then stepped down on to the pathway.

"Is that … is that … her?" he said. He took a few tentative steps along the path, then he sped up, brushing past us. He walked towards Melody's house, stopping at the front door. He held out his arms and said something, but we were too far away to hear.

Old Nina stared at him, then her hand reached for the door frame beside her. She shook her head, once, twice, and then, as if in slow motion, she sank to the floor as her legs buckled beneath her.

"Nina!" called Melody.

The man put his hands on Old Nina's shoulders. There were tears streaming down her face.

"Get off her!" I cried. "What are you doing?"

Nina looked up at me. "It's OK, Jake. It's fine," she said. She turned back to the stranger and put her hands on either side of his face as she looked at him in amazement.

"Oh my goodness. I knew you'd come home. I knew it!" she sobbed.

"What's going on?" said Matthew quietly.

"I kept the lamp on for you, Michael," Old Nina said. "I knew this day would come. I knew it."

Matthew and Melody both took a sharp intake of breath. My heart was racing as I stared at the stranger crouching on the floor.

"You're … you're … Michael?" I said. "But … but Michael is dead!"

"He drowned years ago!" said Melody. "You can't be him."

But Old Nina and the man weren't listening to us.

Nina reached out her arms and the stranger wrapped his own round her in a gentle embrace. And as she patted him on his back he whispered to her softly, "It's OK, Mum. I'm here. I'm back for good. And I promise I'll never leave you again."

Chapter 16

A Reunion

"Nina? Are you OK?" I asked.

Old Nina wiped the tears from her eyes as she nodded. She couldn't stop looking at this man: the stranger who had just announced that he was her long-lost son.

"You look so old now, Michael," she said. "But, my goodness, I'd recognize those eyes anywhere." She held his face in her hands before hugging him again.

"I'm so sorry, Mum. There was an accident and … well, I lost my memory and…"

As the man spoke, his voice kept catching, as if the emotion was too much for him. I felt awkward standing there, but at the same time I didn't want to leave Nina alone with him.

"I was watching the telly and I saw a house on the news and suddenly things started to come back to me," said the man. "The house on TV. That was my house! The house I grew up in. They found a skeleton, didn't they? Anyway, it triggered something and I remembered! And I *knew* that was where I'd find my mum and dad. Where is Dad? Is he here too?"

"Oh, Michael. I'm so sorry. Your dad died a few years ago. He became very sick," said Nina.

Michael's face crumpled and he pressed a fist to his mouth. "Oh my. I'm too late. I'm too late," he said.

Old Nina stroked his arm. "I can't believe you came home. You found me!"

Melody cleared her throat. "So where have you been exactly?" she asked. I think Melody was thinking what I was thinking. Was this man *really* Michael? He slowly stood up and helped Nina to her feet. There were streaks of tears running down his face disappearing into his stubbly beard. I tried to do the maths in my head. If he had disappeared aged eleven all those years ago, he'd be in his forties right now, wouldn't he? He did look to be around that age. And I remembered Michael had dark hair from the photos in Nina's hallway, although this man's hair had some grey streaks running through it. I wondered if he was going to answer Melody's question or not. And then he spoke.

"There was an accident. On the beach," he repeated. He turned back to Nina. "If I had remembered what had happened then, I would have come home, Mum. I promise. But I had amnesia. I didn't know who I was. Or where I lived."

Nina nodded, her cheeks wet, as she stroked his arm. "It's OK, son. It's OK," she sobbed.

Claudia appeared in the doorway. "Is everything all right?" she said. "What's going on, Melody?"

"Nina's son is back, Mum. This is, um, Michael," said Melody.

"M-Michael?" said Claudia.

The man put his hand out and a dazed Claudia reached out hers and shook it.

"I'm sorry to surprise everyone like this," said Michael. "I know it's a lot to take in."

Claudia's jaw dropped. She looked at Michael, then us, then back at Michael again. "Hang on a minute," said Claudia. "You're saying you're Nina's son? The one who died when he was a child?"

The man nodded. "I didn't die. I'm here. Living

and breathing and so, so pleased to be home," he said.

Claudia stared at him, utterly baffled.

"I've already made enquiries about having a DNA test," he said. He turned to us. "I am sure you'll all have doubts right now, but when you see the results then your minds will be put to rest."

Claudia took a deep breath. "Well, this is all rather overwhelming, isn't it?" She put a hand on Nina's arm. "Are you OK?"

Nina seemed calmer than all of us and smiled. "I'm fine, Claudia. This is everything I have ever dreamed of." She took a deep breath. "And thank you so much for letting me stay, but the police said I could go, didn't they? So I think it's time." She reached down and took Michael's hand. "Your room is exactly as you left it. If you would like to stay, that is."

Michael smiled, his eyes filled with tears. "That would be wonderful if you're sure? I was going to find a hotel, but yes. Thank you," he said.

I cleared my throat and Michael looked straight at me. I wanted to be happy for Nina but this wasn't making any sense.

"I'm sorry but … why couldn't you remember

how to get home that day?" I said. "If you'd gone to the police, they would have got you home straight away."

The man smiled at me and flushed slightly. "I completely understand what you're saying. It sounds unusual, doesn't it? Someone coming back like this. But sometimes strange things happen, and I promise you there is an explanation. It might sound incredible, but it doesn't mean it isn't true."

"You can tell us what happened in your own good time, Michael," said Nina. "I am not going to rush you."

Claudia stepped towards Nina. "Do you need me to call anyone for you, Nina? Is there anyone else in your family you need to tell?"

Nina took a shuddering breath. "No, thank you, Claudia. I have everything I need right here. Michael is the only family I have."

Michael gave a small cough. "Well, actually ... Mum. There is one more thing," he said. He shifted from foot to foot and looked nervous almost. "There's someone I'd like you to meet."

He hurried to the car and opened the passenger door. Out climbed a boy, around ten years old, holding one of those folded-up puzzle box toys. His hair was light brown and long and he was wearing beige shorts and a black buttoned-up short-sleeved shirt. He glanced at us, his dark brown eyes meeting each of ours in turn.

Michael put his hands on the boy's shoulders and guided him towards us. As the boy walked, his hands quickly worked at the puzzle box, flipping the shapes this way and that.

"Mum. This is Danny. Danny is your grandson."

"Ohh!" said Nina. She walked forward and threw her arms round the boy. His hands dropped down by his sides. The puzzle box game, in a hexagonal shape, dangled beside him.

A soon as Nina let go, he started fiddling with it again.

"Danny! Let me look at you. I can see the resemblance for sure! How are you?"

"I'm fine," he said. He nodded and then forced a smile.

"It's lovely to meet you. How old are you, Danny?" said Old Nina. Danny looked up at his dad, who nodded. "Go on, son. Tell your grandma," he said.

"I'm eleven," he said. The boy looked at me, Melody and Matthew with interest. Then back down at his toy.

"Hi, Danny. I'm Melody and this is Matthew and Jake," said Melody.

The boy gave us the slightest of nods. "Hullo," he said.

"Well, you are the luckiest boy in the world, Danny, because these three," said Nina, pointing to us, "are the nicest friends you could ever hope to have as neighbours."

Danny dropped his head shyly.

"Right. Shall we get going?" Nina said to Michael. "Claudia, would you mind getting my bag? Michael, would you help with my things?"

"Of course," said Michael, and he followed Nina and Claudia into Melody's house.

Danny watched his dad disappear indoors, then returned to the puzzle in his hands, working the pieces quickly and flipping them this way and that.

"Well, this is a lot to take in, isn't it?" said Matthew to Danny. "Finding a grandma you never knew you had."

The boy didn't look up, his hands moving fast. "It is," he said.

"What is that you've got?" I asked, pointing.

"It's a shape-shifting puzzle box," said Danny. "It

can be manipulated into over seventy shapes. And I know that's true because I've counted them."

"Cool," said Melody.

"What's it for?" I asked. "Do you need to win at something?"

Danny shook his head. "Nope. It's just something I do," he said.

Nina and Michael emerged from the house, Michael with Nina's bag over his shoulder and she tucked her arm into his before they began to walk.

"Come on, you two," she said. "Let's get you home."

Danny paused for a few seconds, twisting and opening the shape and then his fingers turned over and under and the shape altered into a smooth square cube. He held it up between an index finger and thumb, showing each of us in turn, before popping the cube into the pocket of his shorts and following his dad and grandmother to the Rectory.

Chapter 17

Sheila Makes Plans

After everyone left, me, Melody and Matthew stared at each other open-mouthed.

"Did that really just happen?" said Melody. "Michael is alive?"

Matthew and I nodded, pretty much stunned into silence. For years we'd known the tragic story about Nina's lost son. And now here he was, living and breathing and fully grown. It was hard to get our heads round.

"That was … bizarre," said Melody. "Let's meet at yours, Matthew, to discuss it."

"I'll be over in a bit. I'm going to get changed first," I said.

When I got in, Mum was sitting in the lounge. My heart lifted! Maybe having an appointment to see a doctor had made her feel a bit better? There was an old black-and-white film on television, and she appeared to be watching it. For a moment the house felt normal.

"You'll never guess what's happened, Mum!" I said. I sat in the armchair and pulled my school shoes off. "Old Nina's son has come back! Remember Michael? He went missing when he was eleven or something, but apparently he's been alive this whole time! And he's got a son called Danny. Who is Nina's grandson! Can you believe it? He hasn't explained where he's been all these years yet, but he said he was going to take some kind of test to prove he really is him. A DNA test. What do you think about that?"

Mum's head was fixed straight ahead, staring at the screen.

"Mum?" I said. "I'm talking to you. They're both staying with Nina, so you'll get to meet them eventually. Nina was crying and hugging him. It was *well* emotional."

I waited for Mum to turn and gasp, "*What? You*

are joking! Her dead son has returned after all this time?"

But there was nothing. She just sat staring at the telly. And then I realized she wasn't watching the film at all. Her eyes were blank.

"Let me know if you need anything, Mum," I said quietly.

It was scary seeing her like this. Anything would have been better than this silence. Her appointment couldn't come soon enough.

I left her in the lounge and let Wilson out for a wee, then I went upstairs and changed into jeans and a hoodie. I left my school uniform crumpled up in the corner, relieved I didn't have to worry about having a clean shirt for a whole week.

"I'm going to Matthew's!" I yelled from the hallway.

I wasn't sure if Mum registered what I'd said or not but I left anyway.

Matthew got some apple juice from the fridge and poured it into tall glasses. The three of us stood in the kitchen.

"Can you believe Michael has been alive all this time?" said Melody.

"I used to imagine him coming back," said Matthew. "But always as a kid, for some reason. Like he had never grown up."

"Where on earth has he been for – what is it? – thirty years, thirty-five? He can't disappear off the face of the earth and just reappear, can he?" I said.

Melody shrugged. "I know. It sounds mad, doesn't it? But remember what happened with Hal?" she said.

Hal had been a friend of Melody's who she had met when he had been hiding out in an old dilapidated building on the edge of the graveyard last year. His background was really complicated, and I guess it goes to prove not everyone has a straightforward life.

The front door opened and Brian came in from work, letting out a big sigh.

"Ahh, home at last," he muttered to himself, dropping his bag down by the stairs.

"Nina was over the moon, wasn't she?" said Melody. "Can you imagine how that must feel? To have him back after all that time? Hi, Brian!"

Brian came into the kitchen and took a can of cola out of the fridge. "Hi, Melody. Jake. Having who back?" he said, opening the can with a *fizz*. He took a swig.

"You won't believe what's happened, Dad," said Matthew. "Michael is back! Nina's son!"

Brian spluttered on his drink, his eyes bulging. He mopped at his chin with his sleeve. "You what? Say that again."

"Michael is back! From the dead!" said Melody.

"He didn't die, and he's in the Rectory right now," I said.

"And he's brought his son with him," said Matthew. "A kid called Danny."

Brian stared at each of us in turn, his face a picture of shock, and then he grappled to get his phone out of his trouser pocket.

"Sheila? Are you on the hands-free? You'll never guess what," he said, walking off into the hallway.

After Brian had spoken to Sheila he went round to tell Mr Charles.

Matthew found some bags of crisps and we stood leaning against the counter as we ate them.

"I wonder how Nina must be feeling," I said.

"Probably like all her birthdays and every Christmas Day she's ever had have arrived all at once!" said Matthew. "She must be so happy."

I was pleased for Nina but I couldn't help feeling a tiny pang of envy. Would Nina have any time for me now? I'd liked going over to hers. It was peaceful there and calm. Not like home right now. With Michael back, along with a brand-new grandson, perhaps she wouldn't need me any more.

It wasn't long before Sheila burst through the door, followed by Brian and Mr Charles.

"Matthew! What's he like? Tell me!" said Sheila, throwing her coat over the banister.

"He's all right," said Matthew.

Sheila nodded, waiting for more information but Matthew just gulped his drink. She rolled her eyes and turned to her husband. "Do you think we should go over there, Brian? Welcome him home? Oh my goodness. This is incredible, isn't it? Where has he been all these years?" She froze for a moment and frowned. "He's not a conman or anything, is he? You hear about those kinds of things these days."

"That's what I was wondering!" I said. "What if this Michael is making it all up?" I didn't want to see Nina's good news turn bad, but if he wasn't for real, wouldn't that be worse?

"He said he's going to do a DNA test," said Melody. "That's proof enough, isn't it?"

"And if he isn't Michael, then what would be the point of pretending to be her son?" said Brian. "It's not like she's really rich or anything."

"Oh, she's certainly not rich," said Mr Charles.

"And she doesn't own the Rectory; it belongs to the church. They said she could live there after she was widowed. So you're right, Brian. It's not like a trickster would gain anything by lying."

"I'd better go round," said Sheila. "Just to make sure she's all right."

"You can't go barging in at a time like this, Sheila! It's their quiet family time," said Brian.

Sheila nodded, and then her eyes lit up. "I know! We should do a welcome-home gathering tomorrow! Just something in the morning in the street with all the neighbours. Your mum would help with a few cakes, wouldn't she, Melody?" She didn't wait for an answer and turned to Mr Charles. "We could use your trestle table, Mr Charles."

"Of course," he said. "I'll need you to give me a hand, though, Brian. It's right at the back of my shed. Shall we get it out now?"

"No problem," said Brian, and they headed to the front door.

"Don't you go worrying your mum, Jake. I know she'd help if she could. Is she on the mend? She's not answered my messages but I don't want to bother her if she's feeling rough," said Sheila.

"She's still not great," I said.

I wondered how long I could keep this going before somebody guessed something was wrong. But Sheila was already on to the next thing.

"You three will help too, won't you?" she said and we all muttered yes and nodded. "I'll go over and see Claudia and get the ball rolling. And maybe I can get a bit more information about what Michael is like from her. Oh, this is exciting!" She put her coat back on and opened the front door, then turned.

"Matthew? Write a note to Nina, would you? Say we are going to do coffee and cakes at ten tomorrow. And then pop it through her door."

"Do I have to?" he said.

"Thanks, darling!" she said as the door closed behind her.

Matthew huffed and took a notepad and pen from the top of the microwave. "I don't know what to say," he said moodily.

"I'll do it!" said Melody. She wrote the note and folded it in half, writing 'NINA' on the outside.

"I'll post it on my way home," I said, and Melody passed me the note. "Remember we've still got to carry on with our investigations into Preston James."

"Absolutely. Let's get back on to it after the welcome for Michael," said Melody.

I followed Melody out and walked past my house to the Rectory. I unlatched the gate and walked up the pathway, wondering what might be going on inside. Was Old Nina showing Michael the framed photos of him on the walls of her hallway? Or was he looking at his old swimming trophies and remembering when he won them? I caught a glimpse of someone's silhouette behind the net curtain of the big bay window. They were standing by the glowing lamp. It was someone tall, so I guessed it was Michael.

I hurried along the path, not wanting him to think I was being nosy, then pushed open the stiff letterbox, posting the note through. I imagined it fluttering down on to the mat on the other side. As I headed back down the path my eyes darted to the window again. Something had changed. It wasn't until I got home that I realized what it was. I opened our front door and, before I closed it, I took one more look across the pavement to the Rectory. The outline of the figure had gone, maybe to the hallway to see what I had posted. And the lamp that was always switched on, waiting for Michael to return, had been turned off at last.

Chapter 18

A Welcome Party

I was woken at nine a.m. the next day by the sound of a plastic chair being dragged across the close. I got up and peeked through the gap in my curtain.

Sheila was texting on her phone while pulling the chair to the middle of the road where Brian and Mr Charles were positioning a trestle table. Claudia and Melody came out of their house with carrier bags and a large cake tin. Melody took a pink floral tablecloth out of one of the bags and threw it over the table.

I yawned and grabbed some jeans and a T-shirt from my floor.

I knocked on Mum's door and opened it. The room

was dark and I could see the shape of Mum lying in bed.

"There's a welcome-home party in the close this morning," I said. "For Michael. Remember I said he came back?" I watched Mum's shoulders rise and fall as she breathed. I would have given anything to see her turn and smile at me. And to say, *That sounds wonderful, Jake. Shall we go?*"

"Mum? Can you hear me? It starts in an hour. Why don't you get up and have a shower and come too? Claudia and Sheila are out there now setting up. But you don't need to help. You can just sit and have a cup of tea. You'll get to meet Michael and his son Danny. That would be nice, wouldn't it?"

Silence.

"And if you don't feel well, you can come back here. But at least you would have tried. A bit of fresh air might do you good. You haven't been out for days and days. Everyone would like to see you. They've been asking how you are and I just said about the flu and then you had a chest infection, so no one thinks it's anything else." Maybe if I kept talking, Mum wouldn't get a chance to say no. "So much has been going on, Mum. You don't want to miss any more, do you? So can you come? For me?"

There was a deep sigh from Mum's bed. "Not today," Mum muttered.

I felt a tidal wave of rage erupt within the pit of my guts. It rolled up past my chest, making my throat tighten until it was right there in my mouth, and I had no control over it.

"Why aren't you getting up?" I said. "You're my MUM. What is wrong with you?"

I began to pace beside the bed. I could hear my words, but it was like I was watching someone else say them.

"I'm only a kid. I'm not supposed to be looking after *you*. You are supposed to be looking after *ME*! And ... and you're just ... you're just lying there, doing NOTHING. And you're going to lose your job and then we won't have any money. What are we going to do then, eh?" I clenched my hands. I glanced at Mum but she still hadn't moved. "You won't talk to anyone, but where does that leave me? Have you thought about that? Have you wondered how this is affecting *me*?" I stopped walking and stared at Mum's back. She wasn't moving at all. Surely she'd heard me this time?

"Mum? Are ... are you OK?" I said, the anger draining out of me. I placed my hand on her arm and a wave of relief swept through me when I felt her breathing. I sat on the bed and put my arms round her. I began to cry.

Ever so slowly, Mum lifted the arm she was lying on and reached her hand to my shoulder, which she patted. "I'm sorry, Jake," she said.

And then her arm flopped back on to the bed and she tucked her head deeper into the duvet.

I lay there with Mum for a while, listening to her breaths. I felt so exhausted by everything and I wasn't really in the mood for everyone being all happy about Michael's return. But I *did* want to see what he had to say about where he'd been all these years. So I brushed my teeth, got my trainers on and went out into the bright autumn sunshine.

"Hi, Jake!" called Melody from her driveway. She was carrying two large flasks. "How's your mum? Is she getting better?"

I took a breath and for a second I nearly told her everything: how Mum was depressed and that, although she was seeing a doctor soon, she was worse than I'd ever seen her. But then Claudia called, "Melody? Where did you put the teabags?"

Melody hurried over awkwardly with the heavy flasks. "They're in the bag right there!"

Cameron and Kyle came out of number seven, Cameron with a large chocolate cake that he placed in the centre of the table, and Kyle with two wooden chairs.

"Isn't this incredible?" said Cameron to anyone who was listening. "First a dead body in the garden and now a body returned from the dead!"

Kyle gave him a playful slap on his arm. "Cameron! Sshhh. They might hear you." He glanced at the Rectory and then said to Brian, "What's he like, Brian?"

Brian shrugged. "No idea. I've not met him yet." Brian opened two large packets of crisps and shared them out between some bowls.

"Nina must be in a state of shock," said Claudia. "First a skeleton and then getting arrested and—" She stopped talking as the door of the Rectory opened. Old Nina was standing on her step, her hair curled and pinned neatly. She was wearing a bright yellow dress and a white cardigan and she was beaming.

"Ah, here they are!" said Sheila, clapping her hands together.

Michael was behind Nina, dressed smartly in jeans, a shirt and blazer. Danny was behind him in a T-shirt and jeans, the puzzle box spinning in his hands. I felt a lurch in my guts. They looked so happy together.

"It's so lovely to meet you!" said Mr Charles. He walked up to Michael and shook his hand vigorously. "Welcome to Chestnut Close."

"Yes, welcome home!" said Brian.

Everyone took it in turns to shake Michael's hand and he seemed quite overwhelmed with all the attention.

"Would you like a cup of tea, Michael?" said Claudia, positioning herself behind the trestle table.

"Yes, please. That would be lovely," said Michael. He turned around, his hands clenched at his chest. "Wow. This is … well, I never expected this, I must say."

Everyone 'ahhh-d' and laughed a little.

"We thought it would be nice for you to meet us," said Sheila. "I'm Sheila, Matthew's mum. You met Matthew, didn't you?"

Michael nodded. "Yes, and Melody and Jake," he said, pointing at us in turn and smiling. He put his hands on his son's shoulders. "And this is my son, Danny."

Danny shuffled forward, his head down as he played with the box puzzle.

"Hi, Danny!" everyone said.

The young boy nodded and said "hello" quietly.

There was a bit of an awkward silence, but then Cameron said he'd start slicing some cake and everyone relaxed a bit when they had some food and a drink.

"So what exactly happened to you, Michael?" said Mr Charles. "I'm sorry if that's a painful question. But, well, we're all wondering, to be honest."

We all stared at Michael, who was gazing into the distance.

"It was … it was such a strange time," he said. He cleared his throat. "I'm almost embarrassed to say what happened because, well, because it sounds so unbelievable." He laughed, seeming a little nervous.

Everyone had stopped eating and drinking and was transfixed by what he was going to say next.

"As I told Mum last night. Um. On that day, the day I lost my family, I remember walking out to the sea to have a swim. It was a long way, wasn't it, Mum?"

Nina nodded, placing her hand on his arm. "Yes, darling. It was."

Michael carried on. "I went into the water and swam around for a bit. Back then I was a very good swimmer. I'd won lots of competitions."

I knew that from the trophies I'd seen.

"Well, I was swimming around and ... well, there must have been a freak wave or the wash from a speedboat or something. And the next thing I knew I was tumbling over and over in the water."

Nina shook her head. It must have been upsetting for her to hear.

"Everything went black and when I woke up, I was wrapped in a blanket in the bowels of a boat. There was a woman and a man there. I remember the man was wearing glasses and they were speckled with seawater. They said they had found me struggling and pulled me to safety. And they ... they looked after me."

"What?" said Brian. "What do you mean they looked after you?"

Michael rubbed at his forehead. "I know. It sounds odd, doesn't it? And ... well, I don't want you to think badly of them because I know in their hearts they were good, good people. Remember, I had lost my memory at this point and didn't even know my name."

"They took you to a hospital, though, surely? Or to the police?" said Kyle.

Michael looked down at the ground and paused.

Then he took a deep breath before looking up again. "No. I'm afraid they didn't. These people were kind. They really were! They asked me my name, where I was from, but I didn't know."

I frowned. "So you were scooped out of the sea, plonked on a boat and taken away?"

Michael cleared his throat. "I guess you could say that. They gave me a new name – Christopher. So it's strange being called Michael after all these years," he said, smiling almost shyly. "Janet and Harvey lived their lives sailing around the world. They took me to places I could never have dreamed of seeing. But I knew, deep down, that it wasn't where I was supposed to be. I had an instinct inside that I belonged somewhere else. But, well, I couldn't remember where that was."

"Not even when you grew up? Your memories didn't come back?" asked Matthew.

Michael shook his head.

"Janet and Harvey loved me. They always wanted a child and I guess it felt like a gift had been handed to them. And I didn't want to upset them. They were so kind to me."

Everyone was silent, taking in everything Michael had just said.

"That is criminal. Those people stole you! You were kidnapped! You need to report them to the police!" said Mr Charles.

"Yes," said Brian. "I'm sorry, Michael. But Mr Charles is right. What those people did, denying Nina here of years with her son. Well, it's utterly despicable."

Michael closed his eyes and nodded slowly. "I know. But the thing is, there is no point in telling the authorities because they both passed away, within a few years of each other actually. And now I just want to get back some of the time I've lost with Mum." He turned to Nina. "I'm starting to get my memories back a little bit. I think it's because I'm back here, in my childhood home. I remember the Christmases and birthdays. Going on picnics with Dad! Do you remember the day we scraped the wallpaper off my bedroom wall and it kept getting stuck in my hair?" Nina let out a little gasp. Michael gripped her hands with his and I saw Claudia dabbing a napkin at her eyes.

"But it's time to create some new memories, isn't it, Mum?" said Michael.

Nina had a tear trickling down her cheek. "Yes, Michael. It is time," she said.

*

Everyone seemed to relax after hearing Michael's explanation. They all ate cake and drank tea and took it in turns to talk to him and Danny. Matthew, Melody and I stood to one side.

"Sounds kind of believable, don't you think?" said Matthew.

"I think so," said Melody.

"It explains why he hasn't been back, I guess," I said. "And if he gets a DNA test, then there's no reason to doubt him, is there?" I knew I should be happy for Nina, but I couldn't help the heavy feeling in my tummy when I looked at the three of them together.

Just then Michael came over, Danny following on behind.

"Hello again," said Michael. I scrutinized his face, trying to see if there was any resemblance to the boy in Nina's photos. It was hard to tell. Half his face was covered in a beard and his hair was greying at the temples. He did have dark brown eyes, the same as Michael's, though.

"How does it feel to be home?" said Melody.

"It's wonderful," said Michael. He turned to me. "It's Jake, isn't it?"

I nodded.

"I must thank you, Jake, for looking out for Mum,"

said Michael. "She said you've been helping her in the garden and that you found the skeleton? That must have been pretty crazy, huh?"

I stuck my bottom lip out. "Yeah, I guess," I said.

He put a hand on my shoulder. "Well, thank you. She had quite a shock and I know you've been helping her out around the garden. But you don't need to worry about doing any more jobs for her now that I'm back." His eyes fixed on mine, creased at the sides as he smiled.

"Oh, right," I said. "OK." Was he telling me I wasn't welcome at the Rectory any more? Maybe I was imagining it.

Sheila came over and joined us. "What kind of memories are coming back for you, Michael?" she said. "If you're happy to share, of course." Everyone gathered round, wanting to hear more about this miracle man.

Michael sighed. "Oh, so much. So, so much," he said with a gentle shake of his head. He cleared his throat and turned to Nina, who had come to stand beside him. "Do you remember that space hopper you bought for my fifth birthday?" he said. "The big orange one with the smiley face on the front?"

Nina frowned, rooting through her memories. "A

space hopper?" she said. "Um. I'm not sure. Let me think."

Matthew, Melody and I looked at each other. She didn't seem to know what he was talking about.

"I used to bounce around the garden on it. You must remember," said Michael, laughing awkwardly.

We all froze, waiting for Nina to say something.

Nina turned to her grandson. "Danny? Can you run inside and get the large black photo album that's by my armchair, please?"

Danny blinked at her, then ran to the Rectory and through the open door.

Michael looked uncomfortable while we waited and everyone stared at him, not saying anything. I spotted Cameron shrugging at Mr Charles. Then Danny came bombing back with his puzzle box in one hand and the photo album under his other arm. He passed it to Nina who placed it on the table by the teacups. She flicked through the pages, then stopped.

"Ah. I knew I had a photo somewhere. Was it that one?" She angled the page so that Michael could see. It was a picture of a brown-haired Michael sitting on a round orange space hopper in the back garden. He was holding on to two handles, his face beaming in the bright sunshine.

"That's it!" he said, grinning as he took the album. "Oh, look at these. These are wonderful. Look at Dad! He looks so young."

He turned the pages and stopped when he got to a photo of him standing in the corner of the lounge beside a Christmas tree and a pile of presents.

"I remember those pyjamas!" he said. "Was this the Christmas I got the skateboard? And I got a football annual, and some new swimming trunks."

"Yes, I think it was!" said Nina. "You loved that skateboard, didn't you?"

Michael looked up at us. "I used to come out here to play on it. Your houses weren't even built then. It was just the Rectory and a dusty road."

Everyone seemed to breathe a sigh of relief the more memories Michael recalled, laughing and saying things like "Oh, that's wonderful!" and "How amazing!"

The conversations carried on and soon people started clearing up. Michael helped, even though everyone said he really shouldn't. He lifted the trestle table with Mr Charles and they shuffled towards us.

"Shall we go to town in a bit? See what we can

find out about Preston James at the cinema?" said Melody.

I had almost forgotten about that, with Michael and Danny turning up.

"Definitely," I said.

We moved out of the way for Michael and Mr Charles to walk past with the table.

"Matthew? Are you coming to town to investigate?" I asked.

Matthew nodded. "I guess so," he said. "But I'm busy later."

"Doing what?" said Melody.

Matthew shrugged. "This and that," he said mysteriously.

Michael returned and we watched as he went over and said something to Danny who was sitting on the Rectory wall, playing with his puzzle. He listened, then jumped down and the two of them came over.

"Sorry to bother you, but I overheard you were going into town later. Any chance Danny could hang out with you for a bit today? It's not much fun here with me and Mum going over all the old stories."

Danny looked up at us, the puzzle box back into a smooth cube shape.

"I guess so," said Matthew.

"Fantastic!" said Michael. He gave his son a slap on the back. "I'll see you later, Danny. Be good."

"I will," said Danny. And his face spread into a wide smile.

Chapter 19

The Smelly Passageway

We arranged to meet outside Matthew's house and when I went out, Danny was already there, standing on his own. He had changed into a navy zip-up hoodie and one of the pockets was bulging with what I guessed was the puzzle box. I had the feeling he didn't go anywhere without it.

"All right?" I said, joining him. I thought I'd better be nice – he was Old Nina's grandson, after all – even though I wasn't particularly happy he was tagging along. I'd rather it was just me, Matthew and Melody.

Danny sniffed. "What are we going to do in town?"

I wasn't sure what to say. Was it a secret what we

were doing? I felt that Nina wasn't in as much danger of being rearrested now, but I still had a dead man's suitcase hidden under my bed. Maybe *I* could get into trouble for that? The sooner we found out more about what had happened to Preston James the better. Maybe something in the cinema that he used to own would give us answers about who might have wanted him dead?

"We're kind of investigating something," I said. "There's an old cinema on the high street and we want to take a look around."

"Oh, OK," he said. Matthew and Melody turned up and we headed off.

"How are you finding Chestnut Close, Danny?" said Melody.

Danny put his head on one side and seemed to really think about the question. "It's fine," he said. "I like it so far, I guess."

"Where do you live?" said Matthew. "Or are you living here permanently now?"

Danny shrugged. "We live here and there," he said. "I dunno if we're staying." I felt my heart lift a little at that news. Maybe they'd just go back to wherever they'd been after everything had died down.

We walked for a bit in silence.

"It must be nice meeting your grandma after all this time," I said. "Bit weird too."

Danny wrinkled his nose. "I suppose," he said. "But she's very nice and I like her a lot."

We crossed over at a pelican crossing, then continued on towards the main part of the high street.

"So, um, what is it you are looking for at the cinema?" said Danny.

"We're not sure at the moment," said Melody. "There's a bit of a mystery around the skeleton that was found in your grandma's garden. We're trying to find out about the man and how he ended up there."

Danny pulled on the cuffs of his sleeves. "Oh yes. Preston James," he muttered. He looked up at us. "Me and Dad saw it on the news."

We passed the mini supermarket. We were nearly there.

"What would you find out about him in a cinema, though?" Danny asked.

"He used to own it years ago, so there might be some clues there. Paperwork or something," said Matthew. "But, like I've said to these two, we can't exactly walk up and open the door. For a start, they're all chained up. Look."

We stood at the bottom of the cinema steps. The wide doors at the top had a thick metal chain looped through the door handles and secured with a huge padlock. Melody gave the door a rattle. I looked around at the shoppers and people going about their day, but no one seemed to notice.

"Let's go home," said Matthew. "This is a waste of time. We can't break in. We'll get into trouble."

Danny walked on a little way, towards the Magpie pub. He turned back. "There's a passageway down here!"

We hurried over and he was right!

The passageway was extremely narrow. Melody stood at the entrance and spread her arms wide, placing a hand on each of the walls. "It's tiny," she said.

"And smelly. What is that stink? It's disgusting," I said, trying not to breathe in too deeply.

"It's urine," said Melody matter-of-factly.

"Let's hope that's all it is," said Danny, wiggling his eyebrows, which made me laugh. "Are we going to take a look, then?"

Matthew was jittery now, pacing around.

"I think it's worth it. There might be another door down there. Like a fire exit or something," I said.

Melody put on the torch function on her phone and I did the same. Matthew hesitated and put his arm across his face, protecting his nose and mouth with the crook of his elbow. Entering somewhere as dirty and smelly as this would be really difficult for him.

"You can wait here if you want, Matthew," I said. "We'll let you know what's there."

Matthew frowned over the top of his arm, then he shook his head. "I'm coming. But you go first, in case I need to get out," he said, his voice muffled.

Melody went first, then Danny, then me. The passageway got darker and smellier the further we walked. My torch light lit the glistening wet ground, which was quite slippery in parts.

"Eek! What was that?" said Melody. "Something just ran in front of me!"

"A rat maybe?" I called. I heard a stumble behind me. "Are you all right, Matty?" I pointed my torch at him. He was a few paces back, slowly edging along like he was on the side of a cliff. He didn't say anything, but I saw him nod in the gloomy light.

"There's just bins at the end," said Melody.

Danny came to an abrupt stop and I nearly careered into his back.

I pointed my torch beam at the dank, slimy brickwork, slowly moving it around.

"Hang on! Point your torch this way, Jake," said Matthew, removing his arm, then shielding his face again. He was waving his other hand close to where he was standing.

I angled the light and it picked up a rotten wooden door the same brown colour as the bricks. There was a hole where the handle would have been. When Melody nudged it gently with her foot, it opened out into a very dark space.

"Urgh. It looks horrible in there," said Matthew.

"Yeah. It looks like the kind of place people go in and never come out," I said.

"I'm not sure you should go in with us, Danny," said Melody, turning to face him. "Why don't you wait by the end of the alley? We won't be long."

Danny shook his head and I saw his white teeth flash in the darkness. He was grinning. "And miss out on all this fun? No way!"

Then, before any of us could stop him, he stepped into the blackness.

Chapter 20

The Old Cinema

"Danny! Wait for us!" I called. I couldn't believe he'd stepped through a pitch-black creepy doorway. He didn't even have a torch!

Melody and I followed him over the threshold and I shone my torch around.

"Where did he go?" said Melody.

Matthew crept over the doorway after us, still with his arm over his face.

"Danny? Where are you?" I shouted.

"I'm here!" said Danny, coming out from behind a pile of boxes. Even though we had some light from our torches, it was hard to see anything. It stank, but this time of mould and something rotting rather than wee. As well as the stacks of cardboard boxes there were piles of carpet tiles and some upturned cinema seats.

"Anyone for an ice cream?" called Danny cheerfully. In the corner of the room was a little trolley on wheels that had a photo of a big ice cream in a cone on the side. Danny was pulling faces and rubbing his tummy as if he was hungry.

I laughed. Old Nina's grandson was quite funny. I felt another pang of envy in the pit of my stomach. She must be so happy to have him in her life now.

I went over and peered inside the cabinet. It had a sliding glass door on the top that was open. Inside was a bundle of rags and it looked like something had made itself a nest. I wasn't about to root around and see what.

"Can we hurry up?" said Matthew from behind his arm.

"There's a door over there," said Melody. "Let's see if we can turn a light on." She tugged on the door, which opened out on to a corridor.

"Why don't we go and find where they showed the films?" said Danny. "That would be so cool." He really seemed to be enjoying himself.

"Not now," I said. "We're looking for anything to

do with Preston James, remember? Let's see if we can find an office or something?"

Danny huffed but nodded. "OK."

We walked along the corridor, the carpet sticky beneath our shoes. Our torches caught glimpses of framed movie posters and other memorabilia pinned along the wall.

Melody stopped to take a closer look. "Come and see this!" she said. There was a black-and-white photograph of a woman standing on the steps outside the cinema. On either side of her were two men in suits shaking hands. Melody read the caption underneath. "*Cinema manager Harriet Duncan, with owners Preston James and Jed Hyde.*"

Danny pushed his way in front and peered up. "So that's Preston James. And that's Jed Hyde." He pointed at the names beneath the photo.

"It seems Preston James had a business partner," said Melody. "Maybe we can find him and ask some questions? He might be involved in this."

Matthew took his phone out. "I'll look him up. Hang on."

I watched as his eyes widened in the darkness. "Nope. No chance of asking him anything. He died in prison of a heart attack ten years ago."

"Prison? What was he in prison for?" I asked.

Matthew scrolled on his phone. "Burglary, handling stolen goods, that kind of thing. Ah, it says that Jed's wife, Tina Hyde, was also jailed. But she was released a few years back. We could try and talk to her maybe? If we can find her."

"What would we say?" I said. "We can't just go up to an ex-criminal and ask if she had anything to do with Preston being dead in Old Nina's back garden."

"Well, no. We can't ask it like that. But maybe we could—" Melody began. "Hang on. Where did Danny go?"

We looked around and there was no sign of him. We heard the distant bang of a door.

"What is he doing?" said Matthew, panic on his face.

We hurried along the corridor as it bent to the right. At the end was a door with a sign that said SCREEN ONE in faded white writing. I pushed the door and Melody ran to a panel on the wall and flicked a switch. Above our heads were four huge ornate light fittings that flickered to life and illuminated Danny, who was standing halfway along the middle aisle.

"This place is amazing!" he said, his chin high as he took in the surroundings.

"You shouldn't wander off," called Melody. "But, yes, it is pretty special."

In front of us were rows and rows of red padded seats. The floor sloped downwards to a screen that was hidden by a large draped yellowing curtain that hung in swathes of silky fabric.

Danny ran down the slope and along one of the rows. He got to the middle and pulled a seat down with a creak, then he sat in it and spun round.

He grinned. "Look at me! Got any popcorn?"

I noticed that some of the seats were covered in white dust and lumps of masonry. I looked up and saw that part of the ceiling was missing.

Matthew had spotted it too. "I don't think we should be in here. It's not safe," he said.

"Let's get out. Come on, Danny."

But Danny was too busy wriggling around in his seat. "When's the film going to start?" he said, laughing.

"It's not funny," I called. "We've got to leave."

Danny huffed and got up, the seat pinging closed as he walked along the aisle. Some tiny fragments of plaster fluttered down from the ceiling like snow.

"I think we might have disturbed some of the fixtures. We need to get out. Now," said Melody.

"Hurry up, Danny," I said.

Danny reached us and we turned to go, but then he stopped and patted the pockets of his hoodie. "My puzzle box!" he said. "It must have fallen out."

I watched as behind him a large piece of plaster dropped to the floor with a thump.

"Leave it!" I said.

But Danny shook his head and turned, sprinting back to where he'd been sitting. As he ran along the row a shower of dust rained down on to his shoulders, but he didn't seem to notice as he dropped to his knees behind the worn-out seats. There was another sprinkling of dust. The whole ceiling seemed like it was about to collapse. Why wasn't he coming back? I couldn't leave him! I ran towards the row.

"Jake!" Matthew and Melody called together.

I ran my hand along the rough fabric of the back of the seats as I sprinted towards him.

Danny was on his knees, searching. "I can't find it! I can't find it!" he said.

I reached out a hand and got hold of the back of his hood just as he grabbed the puzzle box from the floor. "Let's go!" I shouted, pulling him along.

More pieces of brickwork and masonry began to fall around us.

"RUN!" cried Matthew.

Danny stumbled behind me and I turned and took his arm, dragging him along. We ran through the door, down the corridor, through the storeroom and out into the smelly passageway. Danny started coughing as we made our way through the narrow gap and out into the bright sunlight. I took a deep breath and leaned against the wall of the Magpie pub, panting. Danny was gripping the box in his hand and he had tears in his eyes.

"You should have come back when we told you!" I yelled. "That was really dangerous, do you know that?"

Danny bit his lip and nodded. "I'm sorry," he said. "I was just enjoying myself and … I couldn't leave it behind."

I frowned and stared at the puzzle box in his hands. His knuckles were red from where he had been squeezing it so hard.

"What's so special about that thing anyway?" I said.

Danny dropped his head and began to flip the shape this way and that. His breathing slowed down. It was then that I noticed there was handwriting on some of the sides of the shape. Little notes that had been stuck on. I twisted my head to one side, trying to see what one said.

Matthew spotted them too. "Are there things written on it?"

Danny froze, the puzzle opened in a diamond shape in his hands. I read one which said:

Believe

"What does that mean? Believe?" I asked.

"It's just something my dad did to keep me focused when I get distracted. At school and stuff," said Danny, folding the box into a cube and slipping it into his pocket.

"Like motivational messages?" said Melody.

Danny nodded. "I read them when I'm playing with it," he said. He looked up at me. "That's why I didn't want to lose it. Thanks for coming back for me." He seemed quite emotional.

"Don't worry about it," I said.

"Right, let's get back on track. We find Tina Hyde next, yes?" said Melody.

Matthew wasn't listening as he checked a message on his phone.

"Matthew?" I said.

"Yep. I can't do anything right now, though," he said.

"What? But you're part of this investigation. You can't let us down," I said.

"What are you on about?" said Matthew. "I'm not letting you down. I've got something to do!"

"Well, what is so important that you just … *go*?" I said. "You've been acting really weird lately, Matthew. Me and Melody have both noticed it. Haven't we, Melody?"

Melody scrunched her nose. "Yeah, kind of," she said. "We are a bit worried about you, Matty. Especially after … you know…" She glanced at Danny, clearly not wanting to say much in front of him. "How you used to be."

Matthew put a hand to his forehead. "Am I not allowed to have my own life away from Chestnut Close?" he snapped. "There is a world outside, you know."

I couldn't believe he was being like this, all high and mighty and as if our street was beneath him. I caught Melody's eye. She was frowning.

Matthew huffed loudly, then spread his hands out as if to calm us down, even though we were just waiting for an explanation. "I'm just busy, OK? I'll see you later," he said. And with that he turned and walked off down the street.

Chapter 21

Spying on a Friend

As we walked home, Melody and I went through all the theories we had about what Matthew was hiding. Danny followed a pace behind us, playing with his puzzle box.

"Maybe his OCD has got bad and he's seeing the therapist again?"

"Could be," said Melody. "Have you noticed he keeps tapping his wrist? Do you think that's a new obsession he's got?"

I shook my head. "I have no idea. Why can't he just talk to us about it? We're his friends," I said.

Although I was a fine one to talk. I hadn't told

Matthew or Melody anything about Mum. Not that they'd noticed anything was wrong. Part of me wanted them to know. It would be a relief in a way. But I was also embarrassed about how Mum was behaving. Besides, she had an appointment now, so everything would be OK soon.

Danny trotted to catch up.

Melody gasped. "Maybe he's got some new best friends? And he's going to meet up with them! But he doesn't want us to feel left out so he's keeping it a secret."

"Do you think so?" I said. Matthew was my oldest friend! We'd had our ups and downs, for sure, but we were all right now, weren't we? Maybe that was why he hadn't picked up that there was something going on with me? Because he had other friends in his life?

"As long as he's OK. That's all that matters, isn't it?" said Melody.

I nodded. Although the thought of Matthew having mates we didn't know about hurt a lot. If he went off with them, what would happen to me? I mean, Melody was all right, but Matthew was like the sticky glue that held the three of us together. Without Matthew, me and Melody were just neighbours.

We reached Chestnut Close and I stopped. "Hang

on. I'll see what I can find out about Tina Hyde before we go," I said.

I searched her name on my phone. It brought up loads of people who were clearly too young to be her.

Melody watched over my shoulder. "Preston and Jed looked about the same age in that photo in the cinema," said Melody. "And Preston died twenty-five years ago so that means she'll probably be in her seventies or eighties."

I kept scrolling, not expecting to have much luck, but a few pages down, there was a website for a care home with the name 'Tina Hyde' highlighted in the text.

"This might be something," I said. "*Blossom House Care Home has recently expanded their business with the addition of a two-storey extension at the back of the existing building. Care home manager David Brown said, 'This expansion means we can welcome more residents to Blossom House, where they'll enjoy our exceptional care.' But not all of Blossom House residents felt the same. Tina Hyde has lived at Blossom House for three years and when asked if she was looking forward to welcoming the new residents she replied, 'More old people? That's all we need.' Mr Brown said that Mrs Hyde had a particular sense of humour...*"

"Ha!" said Melody. "That could be her, I guess."

"The home isn't far so, assuming she's still there, it might be worth investigating."

"Can I come too?" asked Danny.

I huffed. I didn't want him hanging around with us all the time. "It's just an old people's home," I said.

Danny shrugged. "Old people are nice," he said quietly.

I wondered if Danny was going to tell his dad about the falling masonry.

"If your dad says you can, then that's fine. But I'm not sure he'll want you to come out with us again, considering what just happened in the cinema," said Melody.

"Oh, I won't tell him about that," said Danny, winking like a wise old man.

The door of the Rectory opened and Michael appeared, dragging an old heavy-looking rug. He struggled with it down the steps then dropped it in the front garden. A cloud of dust puffed up into the air.

"What's going on?" I said.

"Dad's helping clean the house up a bit. For Granny. She's really pleased about it," said Danny.

"That's nice of him," said Melody. "Right, I'm off. See you later."

Nina appeared in her doorway and patted Michael's arm as he went back inside.

"Bye, Jake!" Danny said, and he sprinted to the house and threw his arms round Old Nina's waist. She laughed and pecked a kiss on his head. Michael reappeared with a small table with a cardboard box on top. I sighed. I could have helped Nina in her house. She only had to ask. I watched as the three of them went inside and closed the door. I dropped my chin and headed home.

I fed Wilson, then scratched my neck, remembering my eczema cream would be ready to collect by now. The pharmacy was on the high street and I groaned inwardly that I had to go all the way back there to get it.

Rather than walk I went on my bike. I used to cycle everywhere, including to and from school, but I was getting too big for this bike now so I only used it when I had to. At the bottom of our road I turned right, crossing over to the cycle lane that led to town.

I stopped at some traffic lights and, as I waited for them to turn green, I spotted a boy with his head hung low and his hands in his pockets, walking away from me. I'd recognize that walk anywhere! It was Matthew! He was heading towards the new shopping precinct! Where was he going? The lights changed and I pushed away, then crossed over, jumping off my bike and walking it up on to the pavement. I thought I'd lost him, but then I saw him going into a shop called Bargain Bonanza. I couldn't go in with a bike, so I hovered by the window trying to see what he was doing. He disappeared for a bit, then I spotted him, staring at the items on a shelf. My heart sank when I saw the sign above his head, which read CLEANING ITEMS.

He turned and I quickly headed off. I'd seen enough. It wasn't new friends he was hurrying to meet. His OCD must be bad again – bad enough for him to be secretly buying cleaning stuff like he used to. I pulled my bike away and headed towards the pharmacy.

It looked like Melody and I were right and Matthew was unwell.

Again.

Chapter 22
Blossom House Care Home

Blossom House Care Home was a bus ride away and the next day Matthew, Melody, Danny and I spread ourselves across the back seat of the number 252. I looked at Matthew and tried to see if his hands were red and sore like they were when he was at his worst, but he had pulled the cuffs of his jumper down. I hadn't told Melody about seeing Matthew buying cleaning products. Maybe I should tell Sheila or Brian? But I knew he'd really hate me for doing that. He caught me looking at him and frowned. I looked away. I didn't want him to feel self-conscious as I knew exactly how that felt. I'd used some cream from the pharmacy last night and this morning, and my skin was already feeling less itchy and sore, which was a relief.

The bus pulled away.

Danny was sitting in between me and Matthew and he swung his legs and thumped them against the seat. I watched the puzzle box spinning in his hands and caught a glimpse at another sticker.

Focus

"What does your dad do, Danny?" Melody asked, nosy as ever. "For a job, I mean."

Danny paused for a second, then flipped the box over and back again.

"He's a salesman," he said, not looking up.

"What does he sell?" said Matthew.

Danny bit on his bottom lip and tilted his head to one side.

"Antiques mainly. Old things. He goes to Europe a lot to meet people and do deals."

I nodded. "Do you get to travel with him?"

Danny shook his head. "No. I stay with my mum when he goes away."

I hadn't thought about Danny's mum. I wondered what she was like. Maybe Old Nina would get to meet her too.

We pulled into a stop near the supermarket and a handful of people got on, including a girl around our age wearing a navy-blue tracksuit with auburn hair curled in a bun. She headed towards us.

"Oh, hi, Matthew!" she said. "How are you?"

Matthew sniffed. "Fine, thanks," he said, avoiding looking directly at her.

"Are you going next weekend?" said the girl, holding on to the pole as the bus pulled away.

Me and Melody watched Matthew as he scratched his nose and looked out of the window.

"Um. Yes. I think so," he muttered.

The girl smiled. "Great! See you there," she said. And she swung into a seat a few rows in front of us.

"Who's that?" whispered Melody. "She doesn't go to our school, does she?"

I certainly didn't recognize her.

"No. I don't think so," said Matthew.

"Well, how do you know her, then?" said Melody.

Matthew scowled. "I've just seen her around, OK?" he snapped.

Melody raised her eyebrows at me.

"And what's happening next weekend?" I asked.

Matthew leaned forward and pressed the button for the bus to pull in at the next stop. We were nearly there.

"Nothing," he mumbled, and then he got up and made his way down the bus. We followed but, unlike me, Melody didn't know when to stop asking Matthew questions.

"Is she local? What primary school did she go to? What's her name?" she said.

"Melody! Just leave it, OK?" said Matthew. "Let's do what we came here to do."

Blossom House Care Home was surrounded by a tall red-brick wall. Two black iron gates decorated with orange and black bunting stood open. A steady flow of people were heading inside.

"It looks like something is going on," said Melody.

Someone walked past us dressed as Dracula.

"It's a Halloween fete! I love fetes," said Danny.

I did too. Me and Mum used to go to the summer fete at my primary school each year. Mum would look after the coconut shy with Sheila, and Matthew's dad Brian was in charge of the hook-a-duck. He always let us cheat and we won loads of stuff.

There was a man sitting at a table folding raffle tickets and dropping them into a glass bowl. He was dressed like Frankenstein's monster with a scar drawn on his forehead and a silver bolt stuck on each side of his neck.

"Let's ask that man if Tina's here," said Melody.

We followed her to the table.

"Excuse me?" said Melody. "We were wondering if Tina Hyde is here today. She's one of the residents."

"I know who she is," said the old man, looking around nervously. He nodded his head to the far corner of the lawn. "She's on the tombola. Dressed as a witch, which figures."

"Thank you," we chimed, and we walked away and joined the crowds.

"This looks brilliant!" said Danny. "Can we play on a few things first?" He was practically bouncing up and down with excitement. I sort of wanted to be annoyed with him for delaying us, but he was right; it did look great. Each stall appeared to be run by a care home resident or member of staff in fancy dress. I could see a zombie, a few ghosts and a woman dressed as a pumpkin.

"I don't see why not," said Melody. "Come on."

Matthew, who hadn't said anything since getting

humpy with us on the bus, cheered up when he won some sweets in the shape of vampire fangs on the hoopla. Melody bought a couple of books on the bric-a-brac stall and Danny won a cuddly bat on the 'throw a welly into the cauldron' game, which was a new one on me.

"Where's the tombola, then?" said Melody.

We scanned the grounds and in one corner I could see a table filled with jigsaws, bubble bath, two bottles of lemonade and some plants. Each item had a different number sellotaped to it. "Over there," I said, pointing.

"That must be Tina Hyde," said Matthew. "Crikey. She looks really in character."

Seated behind the table wearing a wide-brimmed black hat and cape was an old woman. Her arms were folded and she had a scowl on her green-painted face. A man carrying a young boy went to the table, but the woman waved her hand and growled and he scurried away.

"She doesn't look very friendly, does she?" said Danny.

"No," I said. "But we've come this far. Come on."

We approached the stall and the woman shuffled in her seat. "What do you want?" she said.

Melody took a coin out of her pocket. "Three tickets, please," she said, putting the coin on the table in front of the woman. The woman looked left and right, then the coin disappeared under her cape. She held out a basket of folded tickets.

"A winner ends in a zero or a five."

Melody took three.

"Hmmm. No, that's not a winner," said Melody, unfolding one ticket. "And this one isn't either."

The woman huffed. "Well, of course it's not! It ain't worth opening that last one, neither. I took the winners out, didn't I?"

"But that's not fair!" said Melody.

The woman snatched the basket of numbers back. "Deal with it," she said.

Just then a man appeared; he was wearing a sweater with a pink 'Blossom House' logo and a name badge that said 'Steve' in white lettering.

"I hope you're not causing trouble, Tina. Remember? We want to see your happy face today, don't we?" He looked at us and smiled.

"Oh, shut up," muttered Tina. "This place is like a prison. But at least in prison I had more fun."

Melody squeaked. We definitely had the right person!

Steve sighed. "I'm afraid Tina isn't quite herself some days. She has a wild imagination. Don't you, Tina? You like to make up stories, don't you, dear?"

He was talking to her like she was a child. But Tina seemed to be able to handle herself.

"I am not making it up. I went to jail, you know. The police were here questioning me just days ago, weren't they?" she snarled.

"Yes, that's right," said Steve as he moved a few prizes around on the stall. "But they said you wasted their time, didn't they?"

Tina practically growled at the man, but he ignored her and headed across the lawn when someone called out his name.

"Why were the police questioning you?" said Melody. "If you don't mind me asking."

Tina's eyes brightened and she shuffled forward in her seat a little. "They dug up a body and they think I know how it got there!" she said, trying not to laugh. "And I do! I didn't tell them that, of course. I can play the confused, frail old lady when I want to." She cleared her throat and put a hand to her chin. *"I'm so sorry, Officer. I don't know if I did know the deceased. Was he my milkman?"* She snapped back out of character. "Pah! They gave up when they realized they weren't getting anything out of me!"

"Why were you in prison?" said Matthew.

Tina pressed her lips together tightly. I wondered if Matthew had asked too much, but it was as if she couldn't resist blurting out all the things she hadn't told the police. "Handling stolen goods," she said, her eyes twinkling beneath the witch's hat. "My husband was a criminal mastermind!"

She must be talking about Jed Hyde! Preston's business partner.

"What kind of stolen goods?" I said.

Tina relaxed into her seat. She seemed to be enjoying herself now. "Oh, all sorts," she muttered. Her piercing blue eyes widened. "But the forget-me-not diamonds were the best. Five of them, there were! Like the five petals of the flower and with a bluish tinge. Big ones too."

"Diamonds? Where did he get those from?" said Danny, leaning his hands on the table.

"Oh, some lord and lady's manor where they were doing 'work'." Tina did a speech mark sign with her fingers, implying that the 'work' that they were doing wasn't really work at all. She began to laugh. "They weren't even looking for them! The lord had one too many drinks and left the safe unlocked, daft ape. And bam! The diamonds were ours. It was in the papers and everything!"

I made a mental note to look it up after we'd finished.

"Rubble and Mix were prolific," said Tina. "They made more from the stealing than the building, mind you. A few dodgy latches on windows and a nationwide network of professional burglars – and away you go! Two businesses in one."

She shook her head as she chuckled. "My Jed was a modern-day Fagin," she said. "Oh, he was a marvellous man."

"Who's Fagin?" whispered Danny.

"A character in *Oliver Twist* by Charles Dickens," said Matthew. "A crook and a thief, basically."

Tina stopped laughing and straightened up. "If Jed hadn't been double-crossed, then I would be sunning it on the French Riviera right now. Not sitting here surrounded by nincompoops trying to win all this tat!" She waved her hand at the stall, knocking over a bottle of bubble bath.

"Who double-crossed him?" said Danny, transfixed by everything Tina was saying.

Tina inspected her long pink fingernails. "The plan was to sell the diamonds and split the money, but Preston stole them and did a runner. The sneaky little so and so."

Melody gasped at hearing the name.

"He packed his family off to somewhere on the continent and, if he'd been smart, he would have gone with them, taken the diamonds and run, but he didn't. Word got out that he was still in town! He'd taken a room in some old house in town and was using a different name. Pretending to be a lodger!"

"The Rectory!" said Matthew.

Tina ignored him, engrossed in her own story. "My Jed tracked him down and ... well, let's just say Jed came out better on that one."

I couldn't believe it! Had she just confessed that her husband was the murderer?

"What happened to the forget-me-not diamonds?" I said. "I guess you never got them if you're sitting here and ... um, not on the French Riviera."

"I don't know, do I?" snapped Tina. "He hid 'em! When Jed paid Preston a visit, he said he was never going to give them up! He said if anything happened to him, his family would know where to find them. Well, something *did* happen to him, didn't it?" She smirked bitterly. "Jed searched everywhere. He tore their office to pieces! Then the police caught up with him and put him in jail for multiple burglaries and that was that. His heart went kaput and bam. He was dead," she said bluntly.

She looked up at us, her eyes narrowing. "Anyway. What are you lot doing asking me questions?" She scowled, waving her hand at us. "Go on. Go away!"

I was happy to leave her to her misery, but Melody stepped forward.

"Just one more thing," she said. "You said Jed didn't know where the diamonds ended up, but do *you* have any idea where Preston might have hidden them?"

Tina pulled her cape round her and shook her head. "Nope. And Preston's wife Kathleen was about as useful as a chocolate teapot, so there's no way she found them either. Besides, she'd legged it to France and was never seen again. All I know is the last thing Preston said to Jed was, 'They're right under your nose, you daft oaf.'" She snarled and then waved her hand at us again. "Anyway, off you go, you lot. Go on. Shoo! Before I put a spell on you!" She pulled the brim of her hat down low and, muttering to herself, disappeared behind it.

Chapter 23

The Puzzle Box

"Well, that couldn't have gone any better!" said Matthew. "She was dying to tell us everything!"

We were waiting at the bus stop to head home.

"Let's have a recap," said Melody. "From the bank card in the suitcase we know someone called Piers Jackson was staying at the Rectory pretending to be a lodger."

"Suitcase?" said Danny. "What suitcase?"

"It was in your grandma's cellar," I said quietly.

Danny frowned, twitching his nose a little. "And what was inside the suitcase?"

"Just some clothes and some wigs and glasses and stuff," I said.

Danny nodded, his bottom lip protruding. I guess he was gutted he'd missed out on that one.

Melody continued with what we'd learned. "Tina said Preston was staying at an 'old house in town' and that he liked a disguise. So our suspicions were right. Piers and Preston *are* the same man."

"And the disguise explains why Nina didn't recognize him in the police photo," I said. "And Preston had a wife called Kathleen. Which explains the 'K' on the ring I found."

"Preston had stolen some diamonds from his business partner Jed. But rather than run away, he hung around for some reason," Matthew continued. "Jed tracked him down and killed him, burying him in Old Nina's garden. But then he got arrested for other crimes and died in jail."

"They ran a business called Rubble and Mix," said Danny. "I remember that bit."

"Ah, yes! Great, Danny. We should look into that," said Melody. "But before Preston died, he stashed the diamonds somewhere."

The bus arrived and the doors swished open and we climbed on. The back seat was taken so I sat next to Danny and Melody and Matthew sat in front of us.

Matthew was on his phone and then he twisted round. "There's an old news story here about the stolen diamonds!" He read the rest in a whisper. "*Five precious gems known as the forget-me-not diamonds due to their blue tint and petal shape, were stolen from the property of Lord Meadon yesterday evening. The rare diamonds are believed to be worth an estimated*" – Matthew choked for a second – "*one point two million pounds.*"

Danny whistled through his teeth. "Wow. That is *a lot.*"

"What else does it say?" asked Melody, fidgeting beside him.

Matthew scrolled through. "Not much. It sounds like the police never found them."

Melody got her phone out then and the two of them dropped their heads as they scrolled. I knew they'd both be distracted now. I use my phone a fair bit, but I get fed up with it a lot of the time. If I'm honest, I sometimes wish smartphones hadn't been invented. Then people might be more interested in each other and the things around them than looking at a screen all the time. Danny took his puzzle box out and began to play with it, which, in my opinion, was much better than a phone.

"Can I have a go at that, Danny?" I asked. I'd seen kids using them at school before. They looked quite cool and I liked the flip-flap noise they made.

"I … um. I guess," said Danny. He flipped the box round until it was back in a cube shape again and held it towards me. "Be careful with it."

The bus jolted as we stopped at a zebra crossing. At first I couldn't even undo the cube shape and Danny started giggling.

"Don't laugh! You play with this thing all the time – you know how it works!" I used the tip of my finger to pop one of the triangles out and then I was away; the box was unravelled and the folds and joins meant it could turn into all sorts of shapes.

Danny watched me closely. "No … not like that. Yes, now twist it. And turn it upside down and then…"

I was useless and couldn't really get it to go into a symmetrical shape. The little notes from Michael flashed before my eyes. It was probably quite a good way to keep Danny motivated at school, considering how much he played with it.

More by accident than skill, I managed to fold a

couple of the sides of the box and it popped into a diamond shape in my hands.

"Ah, there you go!" I said, laughing. "I got a shape at last!"

Danny clapped his hands. "Dad said that one is like a stolen diamond!"

I stared at Danny. That was a strange thing to say. "A stolen diamond?"

Danny sniffed. "I mean a diamond. I was just thinking about what that old woman said."

I passed the toy to Danny and he quickly fluttered it back into a cube shape and put it in his pocket. Then he turned away, resting his head against the bus window.

Matthew twisted round again. "I think we need to hand all this information over to the police now," he said. "Along with the suitcase and the ring you found, Jake."

My stomach sank a little. "Really?" I said.

"Matthew's right," said Melody. "Tina has basically confessed that her husband was a murderer. We can't keep quiet about that."

"I guess," I said. "But won't I get in trouble for hiding the case?"

Melody frowned. "I doubt it. We found items of

interest and are handing them in. It's not like Nina is under suspicion any longer. *And* we'd be telling the police who killed Preston so they should be happy about that."

"I guess I'll ring that police officer who gave me her card," I said. I looked at Melody and Matthew. "Can you be there, though?"

"Sure," said Matthew, and Melody nodded.

I huffed and stuffed my hands into the pockets of my hoodie. "That's it, then. Our investigations are over," I said, almost sticking my bottom lip out like a spoilt kid. I'd been enjoying this time with my friends. It was a nice distraction from things at home.

But Melody was grinning. "We could still carry on," she said.

"Carry on with what?" said Matthew.

Melody tucked a strand of hair behind her ear. "Well, there's nothing stopping us from trying to find the forget-me-not diamonds, is there? No one knows where they are. And this time there really *is* something to find!"

It wasn't long ago when Melody had been fooled into thinking there was a precious necklace hidden somewhere near the graveyard. We all ended up getting involved in that one, but it was a wild goose chase.

"That's true. The diamonds must still be out there somewhere," I said. "Even Tina doesn't know what's happened to them."

"We could find out where Rubble and Mix had their office and start there?" Matthew said.

"It's already been searched," said Danny. "Remember Tina said that Jed had ransacked it."

"But maybe he missed something?" said Matthew. "Hang on." He took his phone out and typed again. "There's an office address for Rubble and Mix. It might be worth a look? If it still exists."

"I'm up for it," I said, and Melody was nodding.

"Yes! We're going to find the diamonds," said Danny.

And, just like that, things were back on again.

Chapter 24

Listening In On A Conversation

When we got back to the close I headed to my house to get the number for the police and Melody and Matthew followed me.

"You'd better wait out here, actually," I said. "You don't want to catch what Mum's got, do you?"

Matthew nodded and took a step back, and Melody frowned but said nothing.

I went in and grabbed the police officer's business card from the kitchen table where I'd left it. Back on my driveway I dialled the number. Melody was practically dancing on the spot and I could tell she wanted to do the talking, which was fine by me. As soon as the police officer answered, I said who I was then passed the phone to Melody. She said we had information about the Chestnut Close murder and that Tina Hyde had confessed that her husband Jed had murdered Preston. She then told them about the suitcase and the ring.

"We think they belong to Preston James," she said. "Also known as Piers Jackson and Paul Johnson, I believe?" She was grinning and clearly enjoying every second. She answered a few more questions about dates and where the objects were found, and then she hung up.

"They're going to send someone to pick them up later from your house," said Melody. Which, I guess, would be fine if all I had to do was hand them over.

When I got in, Mum was in bed but at least she was sitting up.

"Hi, Mum. Would you like a cup of tea?" I said from the doorway.

"A tea would be lovely. Thank you, Jake," she said. Then she closed her eyes as if the effort of speaking had worn her out.

I made Mum's tea, then took Wilson for a walk.

I took a slow amble along the alleyway beside the Rectory. The door of Nina's kitchen must have been wide open because I could hear the sound of laughter over the kettle boiling. They all seemed so happy and again I felt a pang of jealousy. I knew it wasn't fair of me, though. Nina deserved to have her family back. I carried on my way, doing a short loop round the oldest part of the graveyard and decided to give Nina a knock on my way home. Just because her family was there didn't mean I had to stop helping her, did it? Even if Michael had said I didn't need to.

I knocked on the door and while I waited, I stared at all the objects that were now piled up in the front garden. It looked like Michael had been busy. On top of the discarded rug we'd seen him dragging outside were some wooden floorboards and scraps of carpet. There was also an upturned bedside cabinet with a missing drawer, an ancient vacuum cleaner, the dusty old chandelier from the lounge and some upturned buckets.

Michael answered the door.

"Jake. Hello. How can I help you?" he said, folding his arms and leaning against the door frame. Wilson started to pull to get inside, probably looking for his usual biscuit, but Michael put his leg in the way so he couldn't get past.

I tightened his lead round my fist. "I was just checking in on Nina," I said. "Is she here?"

"She's a bit busy at the moment," said Michael. I could hear Danny singing some kind of silly song from the kitchen and Old Nina laughing.

"Is there anything I can help you with?" said Michael, looking at me intently.

"Um. Well, I usually mow Nina's lawn and, well, I didn't do it last time as I was moving the bits of her shed. And then the police were here. So, um, I just wanted to ask if she wanted me to do it for her later."

Michael smiled. "Thank you, Jake. But I can do that now I'm back," he said.

"Oh. OK."

"That will save Mum a bit of money. Because she told me she was giving you cash each week. And quite a large amount too, I believe."

Michael squared up so that he was facing me, his arms still crossed. I felt my face flush. Did he think I was after her money? That wasn't true at all.

"I can mow it for free!" I blurted. "Nina doesn't have to pay me anything. She just insisted. Or I can help in the house. With all this stuff." I waved my hand at the pile.

Michael raised his eyebrows like he didn't believe

me about the money. "It's fine," he said, smiling. "I can look after her. I used to do jobs like this for Janet and Hugo all the time. The people who rescued me."

I felt my jaw drop ever so slightly. "Don't you mean Harvey?"

Michael pursed his lips. "I'm sorry?" He was almost scowling.

"You said Janet and Hugo. But at the welcome party you said they were called Janet and Harvey. You said the man's name who rescued you was Harvey, not Hugo." My heart was beginning to pound in my chest.

Michael fixed his dark brown eyes on mine as he chewed the inside of his cheek. Then he tipped his head back and let out a laugh. "I think I'd know the names of my own carers, don't you? Hugo! It's Janet and Hugo."

Wilson lay down on the ground and put his head between his paws, letting out a little whine.

"Anyway, I'm sure you have other things you need to be doing, don't you, Jake? Goodbye." And he closed the door in my face.

I hurried home, replaying what had just happened. Something was off about the whole conversation. I was *certain* Michael had got the names wrong.

JAKE: WHAT DID MICHAEL SAY WAS THE NAME OF THE MAN WHO RESCUED HIM? IT WAS JANET AND…?

MELODY: Harvey?

MATTHEW: Yeah, Harvey. I think.

I was right! I felt my stomach clench as I wrote back.

JAKE: HE JUST SAID HIS NAME WAS HUGO!!!!

MELODY: Really?

MATTHEW: Maybe we misheard the first time.

JAKE: What, all THREE of us?!

MELODY: Or maybe he just fumbled his words that morning.

MATTHEW: True. He must have been a bit overwhelmed with everything going on.

My friends seemed ready to come up with an explanation, but I wasn't so sure. And there had always been something about Michael that made me feel uncomfortable. It was hard to explain exactly what, but I had the feeling he wanted to get rid of me. Did that have anything to do with me being friendly with Nina? Or was I just envious of them all playing happy families? I didn't know. My head hurt.

A police officer knocked while I was washing up. I handed over the suitcase and the wedding ring to a man who looked the same age as Leo. He put them in plastic bags and wrote on a label on each one, asking me where and when they'd been found. I repeated everything I'd heard Melody say on the phone. He nodded as he noted everything down, saying they'd be in touch with Nina in due course and that they'd arrange taking statements from the three of us.

"Is she in trouble again?" I asked. But the policeman shrugged, saying he didn't know and he was just here to get the stuff.

After he left I found some tins of soup in the cupboard and warmed some up for me and Mum. I ate every drop but Mum only had a few spoonfuls. I washed up a couple of dishes then watched TV until it was dark, and then I let Wilson out for a final wee.

As I stood by the kitchen door I yawned, watching my fluffy white dog darting around in the darkness. He was really interested in a particular patch of grass and for a moment I worried he was going to dig up something gruesome again.

"Come on, Wilson," I said. "It's bedtime."

He ignored me and trotted to the end of the garden and started sniffing. I groaned, slipped on my trainers and headed out to get him. I walked across our lawn and round the washing line still full of pink shirts, and then I stopped. I could hear voices. They were coming from the direction of Old Nina's garden.

I crept to our wall and rested my head against the bricks as I listened. Two voices were speaking in urgent tones, but I couldn't hear who it was or what they were saying. I closed my eyes and concentrated, but it was no good; I'd have to get closer. Before I gave it too much thought, I stepped on to an upturned plant pot and pulled myself up and over the wall, landing with a thump in the alleyway. I paused, waiting to see if they'd heard, but the voices carried on. I crept alongside Old Nina's garden, trying to make as little noise as possible as my trainers scrunched against the gravelly ground. There was a knot of wood missing halfway along the fence and I peered through.

Michael was standing on the patio with his back to me. He stepped to one side and there was Danny, sitting on a garden chair. Michael was pacing back and forth, agitated. I strained to hear what they were saying, but I could only pick out a few words here and there.

"You don't ... me ... trouble ... after everything?" said Michael.

Danny looked upset. He had his puzzle box on his lap. He shook his head. When he spoke his voice was even quieter than his dad's. "... did ... you said..."

Michael had his head turned away from me and I couldn't hear a thing, his arms moving up and down like he was emphasizing. Then he twisted, slightly, and I heard, "... what suitcase? ... the old lady in trouble. Do you?"

I gasped. Was he talking about Old Nina? And if so, why did he call her the 'old lady' and not 'your grandma'? And why did he mention the suitcase?

Michael stopped pacing and wiped his forehead with the back of his hand. He really did seem stressed: his body was stiff and tense. He shook his head a few times, and then Danny started talking and then Michael again and I picked out a few more words.

"… eye on them … that Jake kid … called Harvey … don't want them … see what they are up to…"

Michael paced back and forth a few more times and I couldn't hear anything. And then he stopped again and I heard: "… doing what I said … our diamonds … looking for…"

I gasped, then slapped my hand over my mouth. I tried not to breathe. Michael's back was still towards me and I stayed as still as possible, expecting him to turn round and see my eyeball staring at him through the fence, but then he started walking back and forth again. I let out a breath. He couldn't have heard. My legs were beginning to tremble from where I'd been crouching. Michael went over to Danny and put his hands on his shoulders. He was saying something urgently now, but I couldn't hear any of it. Then Danny gave a shuddering sob and I heard him say, "OK, Dad. I promise."

Just then, Wilson started yapping from our garden and Michael and Danny looked in my direction. I sprang up and sprinted to the wall and scrambled over. Wilson hurried over when he saw me and I picked him up and went inside, closing the door and locking it behind me.

When I eventually got to bed I messaged Melody and Matthew. My heart was still racing.

> JAKE: When you get this, message me IMMEDIATELY. We need to meet URGENTLY.

Chapter 25

Breaking and Entering

The next morning I had two messages waiting for me on my phone.

MELODY: What's so urgent?!

MATTHEW: Yeah. What's going on, Jake?

I replied quickly.

JAKE: Meet me in the graveyard in 10 mins.

I felt sick when I thought about how Michael had been yesterday – first on Nina's doorstep when he was rude to me *and* had got his facts wrong about his carer's name, and later, when he'd been angry with Danny in the garden and mentioned diamonds. There was something wrong about him. I just knew it.

I got dressed and opened my bedroom curtains. It was pouring with rain, so I found my old coat scrunched at the bottom of the wardrobe, then went downstairs to feed Wilson. I ate a banana and leaned against the cooker, staring at the mess in the kitchen. The table was covered in piles of dirty washing that wouldn't fit in the linen basket or the machine and the cream-tiled floor was almost black with dirt. I vowed I'd try and clear up a bit later.

I took a mug of tea up for Mum. She was snoring so I left it on her bedside cabinet. There were only four days to go until Mum's appointment and it couldn't come soon enough.

I put my trainers on and clipped Wilson's lead on to his collar. He stood on the front mat, wagging his tail, but when I opened the door, he hesitated. His nose twitched as he sniffed at the air. He wasn't a fan of the rain.

"Come on, Wilson," I said. "Let's go, shall we?"

The curtains of the Rectory were still drawn, and I glanced at the ominous black door as I hurried towards the alleyway. Matthew was already there, his hood up and his shoulders hunched forward.

He yawned when he saw me. "What's going on?" he grunted.

Melody hurried along behind me with Frankie under her arm. Frankie hated the rain more than Wilson did. When Melody joined us, I began to explain.

"I heard Michael and Danny talking in the garden last night. They sounded suspicious."

"Why? What did they say?" said Matthew, stifling another yawn.

"I couldn't hear everything, but Michael said my name and 'Harvey'. He sounded angry. I think he was annoyed I'd called him out about getting the name wrong."

I waited for Matthew and Melody to gasp or react in some way, but they didn't seem as shocked as I was. I looked up at the back of the Rectory. A curtain was being pulled open.

"It's not safe to talk here. Come on," I said. I hurried down the alleyway to the graveyard. There was a smell of fresh, wet vegetation in the air.

Everything looked shiny in the rain and big fat droplets were dripping off the orange and yellow leaves of the trees.

"Maybe Michael was just telling Danny about the conversation you'd had," said Matthew. "There's nothing suspicious about that."

"Yes. He could have just been talking about the Harvey and Hugo mix-up," said Melody.

"It wasn't a mix-up! He's lying. I'm sure of it. And they weren't just having a chat – Michael was angry! He was pacing and Danny was upset."

Matthew and Melody frowned at each other. "Also, Michael called Nina 'the old lady'," I said, almost panting to get it all out. "Why would he call her that and not 'your grandma'?"

"Maybe you heard wrong?" said Matthew.

"No, Matthew. I didn't," I snapped. "They were whispering too, as if they were worried Nina might hear."

"Nina could have been asleep and they didn't want to wake her," said Melody. "Was it late?"

I pulled the zip higher on the front of my coat. "Well, yes. But it wasn't that kind of whispering," I said.

Matthew snorted. "*That kind of whispering?*

What does that mean? Can you get different kinds of whispering?"

He laughed and I glared at him. "You weren't there, Matthew! I'm trying to tell you that the way they were talking, or whispering, made them sound guilty, all right? I don't think Michael is who he says he is."

It wasn't much proof, I know – just a few words and odd comments and some tense body language. But it didn't feel right to me. And I was worried for Nina, too. Did she have an imposter staying in her house?

"Look, Jake. I'm sure it all looked and sounded strange," said Melody, "but what about how he remembered all those things about his childhood at the welcome-home party? The Christmas presents and the space hopper? And there's the DNA test he's having too. He seems to be telling the truth to me."

We stopped under the shelter of the old horse chestnut tree and I sat down on the damp bench. The green spiky cases from the tree littered the path and I could see a few shiny conkers peeking out through the splits. Any other time I'd be rushing to pick them up and put them in my pocket, but right now I had other things to think about.

"There's one more thing. He knows something about the diamonds," I said, remembering.

"Diamonds?" said Melody, sitting down beside me. "What did he say?"

I thought back to what I'd heard. "He said 'our diamonds' and 'looking for'," I replied.

Melody took a sideways look at Matthew, who shrugged.

"OK. That does sound weird," he said. "But Danny must have just told him what Tina said."

"I know, but *our* diamonds?" I said. "Why say it like that?"

"I guess that is a bit suspicious, for sure," muttered Melody. "What *is* going on?"

"Maybe we should go to the police again," said Matthew. "Tell them about Michael suddenly turning up and let them sort it out."

"But there's no proof," said Melody. "They might be suspicious that Michael is back, but so what? Nina has willingly let him into her home, welcomed him with open arms. He hasn't done any harm."

Melody was quiet as she picked Frankie up and put him on her lap, stroking his soft ears. I could tell she was thinking it through.

Matthew slumped on to the bench beside me. "If

he isn't for real, Nina is going to be devastated," he said. That was the biggest thought in my head too. How would Old Nina cope with such awful news? But surely it was more important that she knew the truth?

"Maybe we can talk to Danny?" said Melody. "If he isn't really Nina's grandson, he might let something slip about what they're doing here and what they know."

"He'd be sworn to secrecy. I can't see him giving anything away," I said. "But there's something else we can try."

"What?" said Matthew.

"We go back inside the Rectory," I said.

Matthew huffed. "Again? But we can't do that! Nina never goes out so there's not going to be any chance anyway." I looked at Melody and she had a sly smile on her face.

"She's going out today, though," she said. "Mum said Michael and Danny are taking Nina for lunch."

"That's our chance," I said. "We keep an eye on the house, and then we get inside and see if we can find out what this Michael person is up to once and for all."

"Agreed," said Melody.

"OK," said Matthew. "But I'm not happy, you know? I'm not happy about this at all."

"When are you, Matthew?" I said, smiling.

He shook his head and laughed.

We took it in turns to keep an eye on the Rectory for any sign of movement and then, at exactly midday, Matthew messaged.

MATTHEW: WE HAVE LIFT-OFF.

I peeked outside and saw Michael opening the passenger door of his car for Nina. She was wearing a navy dress and a smart pink jacket. Her face was beaming and my heart sank to think this could all be a lie. Danny came out of the house and closed the door behind him, skipping down the path and climbing into the back seat of the car. There was something different about him but I couldn't put my finger on what it was. Maybe it was because I saw him as a fake now and not the person he was pretending to be. The car engine started and Michael made a slow circle round the close before driving off down the road.

I went downstairs, counting to five before opening the front door. Matthew and Melody were also coming out of their houses and we met at the Rectory. Matthew's eyes kept darting around, clearly checking if anyone was watching us.

"I feel really bad about this," said Matthew. "It was different the other day because Nina specifically asked you to go to the cellar. Now we're just breaking and entering."

"I know," I said. "But this is important. We're trying to stop her from being conned, remember?"

"She won't know, anyway. They'll be gone for ages," said Melody.

On the Rectory's steps I moved the plant pot where the key had been before, but now all that was there was a family of woodlice.

"Bum!" I said.

"How are we going to get in without a key?" said Melody.

"Come on, hurry up!" said Matthew, jiggling around. "Someone might see us!"

I thought for a moment. "Let's go round the back," I said.

We ran down the alleyway and I climbed over Nina's fence. Melody followed, landing on her toes, then Matthew dropped down, brushing dirt from his hands.

Melody ran to the back door and gave it a tug. It was locked. The cat flap popped open and Pepper came out, miaowing loudly. Melody crouched and gave her a stroke and the cat stretched her head up high to meet her hand.

All the windows were shut and I cupped my hand round my eyes and peered into the kitchen. "Come on, Melody. You're clever. Think! How can we get in?" I said.

Pepper sauntered off, then sat underneath the garden table and licked her paw.

Melody stared up at the back of the house and tapped her lips with her finger. "There's an open window up there. You can climb the drainpipe, shimmy along the ledge then climb in! Easy!"

I looked up. "You *are* joking, aren't you?"

She shrugged. "It was just an idea." She crouched down and peered through the keyhole of the back door.

"The key is still in the lock," she said. "If we push it through it'll drop on to the floor and then we can put a hand through the cat flap and pick it up!"

"That's more like it!" said Matthew.

Melody tried pushing her little finger into the gap.

"We need something thin to push it through,"

she said. "The key is twisted slightly so it needs to be straightened up first."

The three of us looked around to see if there was anything we could use on the floor. Maybe a small stick or something?

"What about this?" said Matthew, nudging something with his foot. It was a long rusty-looking nail that could have fallen out of the old pieces of shed I'd moved. That felt like ages ago now.

"That looks perfect," I said, picking it up and brushing off the dirt. I knelt down and tried it for size in the hole.

"Now try and wiggle it around and line the key up straight," said Melody.

"Yes, Melody. I know what I'm doing," I snapped. I carefully poked the nail round the edge of the key and twisted it.

"Slowly or you'll turn it round even further!" said Matthew.

I paused and glared at him.

"Sorry. Carry on," he said.

I took the nail out and put my eye to the hole.

"That's it. It's lined up. I just need to push it out now."

I put the nail back in and eased the key backwards.

It moved slowly and then there was a jingle as it landed on the tiled kitchen floor.

"You did it!" said Melody. "Well done, Jake." She dropped to her knees and pushed open the cat flap. "I can see it!" She stuck her hand in through the flap right up to her shoulder. Matthew watched through the window on the kitchen door.

"That's it! More to your left. A bit more. You've got it!"

Melody pulled her arm out with the golden key in her hand. She put it in the lock, turned it, and we were in.

Chapter 26

Snooping Around

We stepped into the kitchen. It looked exactly like it had before, but now there were three place mats at the table rather than just one. A tower of photograph albums balanced on a chair and I imagined they must have been looking through them together over dinner.

The hallway was chock-full of bits and pieces from the lounge. Old Nina's armchair was by the stairs, piled high with the swimming trophies and model planes from the shelves. I poked my head round the lounge door.

"Whoa. Look at this!" I called.

Matthew and Melody joined me.

"Michael really has got into his renovations," said Matthew.

The furniture and carpet had gone and there was a wire dangling where the old chandelier once was. Some of the floorboards had been taken up too, and there was a hole in the ceiling.

I peered up into the darkness of the floor above. "Bit weird, isn't it? What has he actually done apart from make a mess?"

"Maybe there was a leak upstairs?" said Melody.

I supposed she could be right. "We should look in Michael's old room and see if he has left anything like a passport or something," I said. I went out to the hallway and took the stairs two at a time, waiting for Melody and Matthew on the landing. The door to Michael's room was closed and I pushed it open.

"Wow. Someone's made themselves at home," said Matthew. The room, which before had been immaculate, was a complete mess. There were clothes strewn all over the floor, four half-drunk mugs of tea on the carpet by the unmade bed and crisp wrappers and old socks on the desk. I picked up the stuffed gorilla and an empty coke can and put them on the desk.

"What a state," I said. "Even my room isn't this bad. Right, come on. Let's start searching." There was a sports bag by the window and I put it on the bed and unzipped it. It was full of clothes. I moved some jeans and tops to check the corners. Nothing. I put the bag back where I'd found it. Matthew checked the drawers of a bedside table and Melody looked in the bookshelf.

"I was thinking," said Matthew, "even if we find he has ID with a different name, then won't that just be the name the couple gave him? Christopher, wasn't it? And won't it be fake anyway if they didn't tell anyone about him?"

"Maybe. But at least we can investigate him a bit more if we have a surname. See if his story stacks up," I said, checking under the pillow.

Melody opened the wardrobe and took a sharp intake of breath. "Oh my. These are all Michael's clothes from when he was young," she said, running her hand along the line of T-shirts, jumpers and jackets. She turned to us. Her forehead was creased. She looked upset. "I'm not sure we should be doing this. It's just so sad."

"We are doing it for Nina, remember?" I said. I looked at the clothes then noticed something tucked beneath them. "What's that there?" In the corner was a small cardboard box with 'PRIVATE' written on the side in childish black letters.

Melody pulled the box out. Inside was a pile of hardback books. Each one had a year on the spine.

"They're diaries," I said. "It looks like the young Michael wrote one each year since he was little."

"We definitely can't look at those," said Matthew. "That would be too much. It's not the young Michael we are investigating."

"Yes. Put them back, Melody," I said.

Melody pushed the box back into the corner of the wardrobe and we carried on with our search. I went to the bed and lifted the overhanging duvet to check underneath. I knelt and peered under the bed. There were some old board games, a *Star Wars* jigsaw, a dusty wooden guitar and a football. I was about to get up when I spotted an open book, placed face down at the pillow end of the bed. I picked it up. There was a sticker on the front.

MY DIARY
1984
BY MICHAEL FENNELL

"Look at this!" I said. I turned the cover round so they could see. I thought it was important to know what Michael had been reading so I opened it and flicked through the pages. I stopped. "Listen," I said and began to read. "*Third of June. I helped Mum and Dad strip some wallpaper off in my bedroom today. It was so funny because it kept getting stuck in my hair!*"

I looked up at the others. "Do you remember he said about that when we had the welcome party?"

I flicked further on in the book. "*Twenty-fifth of December,*" I read. "*Today has been the best Christmas ever! I got a skateboard! I never thought I'd get one, but it came! I had a go on it outside, but it is REALLY hard so I'm going to have to practise a lot. It's nearly as good as getting that orange space hopper when I was five. HA! That was brilliant! I wonder what happened to it? I'll ask Mum and Dad tomorrow. I also got some swimming trunks and a football annual, which I'm going to read RIGHT NOW.*"

I looked up at Melody. Her eyes were wide, her lips pursed.

"This is how he knows Michael's memories!" I said. "He's been swotting up by reading Michael's diaries."

"But what if he was just reading his old diaries?"

Matthew said. "It doesn't mean he's guilty of anything."

"Hmmm," I said, not convinced in the slightest.

I put the diary back exactly where I'd found it. Lying on the end of the bed was a pin-striped blazer. I picked it up and checked the pockets. There were some keys and a packet of chewing gum in one pocket and nothing in the other. I checked the breast pocket and took out a folded handkerchief. Fortunately it looked unused. In the corner, embroidered in blue thread, were the initials 'L. J.'.

"That's weird." I held up the handkerchief to show the others. "Why 'L' and not 'C' for 'Christopher'?"

I spotted something under the pillow on the bed and went over. It was a pair of grey silk pyjamas, almost identical to the ones in the suitcase in Nina's cellar. Although these had 'L. J.' on the collar.

Matthew and Melody both stared at the pyjamas.

"Didn't Preston have a pair like those?" said Matthew.

"He did," I said. "Isn't it a bit weird they're so similar?"

Melody chewed on her lip as she thought it over.

I took a breath. Suddenly things seemed to become clearer in my mind. I *think* I'd started to work it out.

"Listen. I've got an idea about what might be going on," I began, almost not wanting to say it out loud.

"Go on," said Matthew.

I swallowed. "I think Michael knew about the hidden forget-me-not diamonds *before* he arrived and he has some connection to Preston James. I think he's here on Chestnut Close to look for clues."

Melody let out a sigh and Matthew scratched his head.

"So you're saying Nina's son knows that Preston hid some diamonds?" said Matthew.

I shook my head. "No. I'm saying that he isn't Michael at all. All that talk of doing a DNA test is a lie. I think he's an imposter and he could be dangerous," I said. "He's not doing DIY or helping Nina tidy up her house. Look at the missing floorboards and the hole in the ceiling downstairs! That's not helping! He's searching for something! The forget-me-not diamonds!"

Melody looked at Matthew, then back at me. A gust of wind made the window shudder and we all jumped.

"Let's take a quick look in Danny's room then get out of here," said Melody.

I put the handkerchief back in the jacket pocket and dropped the blazer on the bed.

Danny's room was much tidier and there was a pile of clothes neatly folded on a seat next to a small bed. On the pillow was Danny's puzzle game in its cube shape. *That* was the thing that was different about him when I saw him getting in the car! He hadn't been holding the puzzle box. I picked it up and began to flip the pieces around. The handwritten notes flashed in front of my eyes. **BELIEVE! TRUST IN YOURSELF!** And then I stopped. There was one I hadn't seen before … **KEEP THE SECRET!**

"Look!" I showed Matthew and Melody. "*That's* not a note to keep Danny on track at school, is it? *Keep the secret*? It's his dad telling him to keep quiet about whatever they're up to! I reckon he's been using him to spy on us. He was very keen for him to come to town with us when we went to the cinema, wasn't he? And Danny wanted to come to the care home."

"This looks bad," began Matthew, shaking his head. He was about to say something else, but he stopped. There was a sound downstairs that made my heart thump like a fist pounding in my chest. Someone was coming in through the front door!

Melody put her finger to her lips to 'shush' us, even though we hadn't said a word.

Downstairs we heard Michael and Danny.

"How on earth did you forget it? You carry that blooming thing everywhere!" said Michael.

"Sorry, Dad. I was rushing to get ready," said Danny. "I won't be long!"

There was the steady thud of footsteps coming upstairs. I looked at the unravelled puzzle box in my hand and threw it on the bed and the three of us scanned the room for somewhere to hide. Matthew opened the wardrobe and climbed in, and Melody dropped to her stomach and shuffled under the bed. There was nowhere left for me! All I could do was stand in the space behind the door and hope he wouldn't spot me.

The door flew open and banged me on the nose and I had to bite down on my lip to stop myself from yelling out. On my right I could see the reflection of Danny in the dressing-table mirror. He stood by the bed and picked up the puzzle box. He was clearly confused as to why it wasn't in a cube like he'd left it. I kept as still as I could. If he looked in the mirror, he'd see me hiding! He turned very slowly and then—

"Danny! HURRY UP!" called Michael.

"Coming!" Danny called back. Then he ran out of the room, slamming the door behind him.

We all waited until we were certain they'd left and

then Melody eased herself out from under the bed and I opened the wardrobe for Matthew.

"He saw his puzzle box had been touched," I said. "Do you think he'll tell Michael?"

"Or whoever Michael really is," said Matthew.

I felt a sense of relief. My friend believed me. I looked at Melody.

"You were right, Jake. Something is going on and we probably need to do something about it," she said.

"Let's get out of here first," I said.

Chapter 27

Questions, Questions

We headed to Melody's house and went to her kitchen. She put the kettle on and got some sachets of hot chocolate from the cupboard. She didn't bother asking us if we wanted any – of course we did. While the kettle boiled, she took three large brown mugs from the cupboard.

"This is pretty awful, you know," said Matthew. "If that man is a fraud, then what about Nina?"

"We need to be one hundred per cent certain before we go to the police," said Melody. "Those business cards, a bit of DIY and overhearing a few words isn't enough."

We each took a mug of hot chocolate and I blew on mine to cool it.

"I think we should ask Nina why she was so keen to keep that suitcase a secret," said Melody. "Does she even know the police have it, Jake?"

"No. And I'm not sure she's going to like it, either," I said. "I'll talk to her and then I can see how things are with Michael too. I'll have to do it when she's on her own, though, which'll be tricky. He clearly didn't want me to talk to her yesterday."

Melody slurped her drink, leaving a line of brown foam on her lip.

"We could create some kind of distraction," said Matthew. "Something that will get Danny and Michael away from her."

Melody wiped the hot-chocolate moustache from her face. "I know! We'll tell Mr Charles that Danny and Michael really want to see his garden. Mr Charles loves showing off his garden. He won't be able to resist letting them in. Then all we need to do is tell Michael that Mr Charles has invited them over. Easy!"

Melody was good at this kind of thing. But Matthew could see an issue. "Nina will go with them," he said.

I remembered how, when Nina had arrived on

my doorstep with the casserole dish, she'd offered to help me if I needed anything. Maybe I needed her help now?

"I can distract Nina," I said. "And when she's out of earshot of Michael and Danny, I'll ask her about Preston and Michael and tell her about the suitcase."

"Brilliant!" said Melody. "I love it when a plan comes together. Let's go and see Mr Charles now."

"Hang on, I haven't drunk my hot chocolate yet!" said Matthew, picking it up and taking a big slurp.

We finished our drinks and headed to number eleven. It took him a while but eventually the door opened and Mr Charles was standing there holding a newspaper. He looked surprised to see us.

"Hello, Mr Charles," said Matthew. "How are you today?"

"Um. Yes. I'm fine, thank you, Matthew," said Mr Charles. He seemed a bit dazed, and I wondered if the doorbell had woken him up and he hadn't been reading a newspaper at all.

"We were just thinking," I said. "You know that Michael and Danny are staying on the close? Well, Michael is interested in gardening and Danny really likes fish. So we thought you could ask them over?"

Mr Charles looked confused. "I'm sorry, Jake. What are you talking about?"

I cringed. This wasn't going to work!

"Do you still have fish in your pond, Mr Charles?" interrupted Melody.

Mr Charles twitched his nose. "Well, yes. Yes, I do."

"Danny really wants to see them! The fish," Melody blurted out.

Mr Charles nodded and folded the newspaper, tucking it under his arm. "Right. OK. Well, that's fine. Tell him to give me a knock tomorrow when I'm not so busy," said Mr Charles, clearly wanting to get back to his nap.

"Um. Danny asked if he could come over this afternoon when they get back from lunch," said Melody. "And Michael really wants to see your garden."

Mr Charles frowned. He didn't seem to be falling for it and put his hand on the door to close it. "That's nice but I'm rather—"

"Michael said your front garden is the best he's ever seen!" I said. "He said he wishes he'd been here in the summer when the roses were out."

Mr Charles paused. "Did he? Oh, that's very kind. What a nice man." He looked over our shoulders at the rose bush that lined his pathway. In the summer it looked like it was dappled in candyfloss from the hundreds of pink roses. "What a shame he couldn't see them in their full glory," he muttered to himself.

"We'll bring them over later. Thanks, Mr Charles. Bye!" said Melody, and she grabbed me and Matthew by our arms and pulled us away before Mr Charles could object.

"That went well," said Matthew sarcastically as he unlocked the latch on the gate. "He clearly doesn't want to be disturbed this afternoon."

"It doesn't matter now, does it? He won't turn them away, not when he knows how keen Michael is on roses," Melody said, giggling.

"When they get back from lunch, we'll leave it half an hour, then knock and tell them Mr Charles has invited them over," said Melody.

"Sounds good to me," said Matthew.

"And as you go past my house I'll come out and distract Nina," I said.

"Fantastic. Good luck, team!" said Melody, giving us a thumbs up, which made Matthew visibly cringe.

Michael drove back on to the close about forty minutes later. I waited another thirty minutes then checked out of the window. There was no sign of Melody and Matthew yet. I heard my name being called. It was Mum.

I ran upstairs to her room.

"Yes?" I said.

Mum was sitting up in bed, still in her dressing gown.

"Jake, could you get me a glass of water, please?" said Mum. The glass on her bedside cabinet was empty. I grabbed it and went to the bathroom to fill it up, annoyed she couldn't even manage this small thing for herself.

I went back to her room and put it down. "There you go."

Mum took a sip. "How are you doing, Jake? Is everything OK?"

She wanted to talk *now*? *Really*?

"I'm fine," I snapped.

My phone lit up.

MELODY: GO! GO! GO!

I watched from Mum's window as Matthew and Melody came out of their houses, walked to the Rectory and knocked.

"And what about … the people outside?" said Mum. "The ones watching us. They … they haven't said anything about taking you away, have they?"

I spun round. What was she talking about? Mum was trembling as she took another sip of water.

"What people, Mum?"

Mum rubbed at her forehead. "There are people out there watching the house. You must have seen them! They're everywhere! They're watching. And they … they think I'm a bad mother. They're going to take you away." She started to cry.

"No one is watching the house, Mum. You're imagining it!"

I went back to the window and Matthew, Melody, Michael, Danny and Nina were outside Mr Charles's front garden. Matthew hung back, staring at my house. I had missed them!

"Everything is fine, Mum. I'll be back in a minute," I said.

I ran downstairs and out through the front door and down my driveway. Matthew was walking backwards, shrugging in a 'where were you?' kind of way.

"Nina!" I called.

Everyone stopped and turned round.

"Can you help me, please?"

I walked towards them and Nina let go of Michael's arm. I could feel my bottom lip beginning to tremble. What Mum had just said had frightened me. Not because I believed her, but because she must be really poorly to be imagining things.

"Hello, Jake," said Nina brightly. "We're going to see Mr Charles's garden and his fish. He's asked us over! Isn't that nice?"

I nodded and wiped away a tear that had escaped down my cheek.

"Are you all right, Jake? Whatever is the matter?" said Nina. Her concerned face made me feel even more upset.

"Could you…?" I felt a choke and stopped. I cleared my throat. "Could you come with me for a moment?"

I saw Matthew and Melody look at each other, probably thinking I was very good at acting.

"Of course. Shall I give you a knock on my way home? Is that all right?" she said kindly.

A little sob escaped my lips then. I was upset about Mum, but the thought that Nina might lose her child all over again made me want to cry. There was nothing I could do about any of it.

"I need you now. Please?" I said quietly.

Michael stepped forward and I tried to avoid his eyes. "Anything I can help with?" he asked. Danny was chewing on his cheek, his brow furrowed.

"No, thanks," I said. "I was asking Nina."

"I'll come now," said Nina. She turned to Michael and patted his arm. "You carry on, love, and I'll be with you in a few minutes."

"Great! Let's go," said Melody.

Michael stared at me for a few seconds, then turned away and they carried on towards number eleven. It had worked!

We took a slow walk back to my house. I pushed open the door and caught sight of Mum at the top of the stairs. She spotted us coming in and hurried away to her room. Thankfully Nina didn't see her.

We headed down the hallway. I'd forgotten what a mess the kitchen was and saw Nina's eyes widen.

"Now, what is it, Jake?" said Nina. "Did you want to talk to me about your mum? How is she doing?"

I bit lightly on my lip to try and stop myself from crying. "Mum's OK. She's going, um, to the doctor on Thursday," I said.

Nina nodded and watched me, carefully. "Are you sure she's OK, Jake? You look a little bit upset."

Nina had a way of being so calm and nice it was hard to hide things. I went over to the sink, moving a few pots around.

"I'm fine," I said. "But actually, I need to tell you something, Nina. About … about the suitcase." I turned back, leaning against the kitchen counter.

"Oh," said Nina. She sat down on one of our kitchen chairs.

I took a deep breath. "I handed it over to the police."

"I see," she said.

"The police know who killed that man so they won't worry you any more," I said. "But they might come back to ask a few questions about the suitcase."

Nina nodded, her shoulders dropping. She'd probably hoped her time talking to the police was over.

"Why was it hidden in your cellar, Nina? And why did you want me to hide it? It belonged to your lodger, didn't it?"

Nina rubbed her chin with her hand and sighed as she nodded. "Yes. You're right. Piers Jackson was his name. After they found the skeleton the police kept asking me if I knew that man. The man they found buried. They showed me his photograph but I had never seen him before in my life. The man in the photo had a receding hairline, whereas our lodger, Piers, had a thick head of hair. I think they thought I was hiding something." She hung her head.

"Piers Jackson was wearing a disguise. We found some props in the case you asked me to hide. You wouldn't have recognized him as Preston," I said.

Nina let out a sigh. "Well, I'm not surprised, I suppose," she said. "Looking back, I see there was something strange going on."

"What was he like?"

"He was only with us for a few months and kept himself to himself. But he was always hurrying in with little boxes or packages of things. He stayed in his room the rest of the time."

"What was in the boxes and bags?"

"I don't know. We never asked and I wasn't one to pry," said Nina. "Then one day he just … vanished into thin air. He had missed two or three months' rent so we assumed he'd run off to avoid paying his bill. A few things had gone missing in the house, you see, and we'd had our suspicions, but we couldn't prove it."

Poor Nina. He was stealing from them right under their noses!

"When he didn't come back, I packed up his clothes and put the case into the cellar in case he ever returned to pay his bill. I forgot all about it."

"Why didn't you hand it over to the police? And then why ask me to hide it?"

Old Nina bit her lip. "I panicked, I suppose. Being arrested was just the most terrible thing, Jake. A man's body was found in my back garden! A dead man! And when I was released, I remembered it was there and I worried that maybe it *did* have something to do with Preston. Then if the police came back, they'd find it and think I had deliberately kept it a secret. I was scared! I didn't mean any harm."

It did make sense, what she was saying. I could see why she was worried about getting into trouble after everything she had been through.

"Is there anything else you remember about him? Anything he said or did? Did anyone visit him at all?"

Nina shook her head. "No. No one visited. But I do remember something that happened a few weeks before he disappeared. He had become quite agitated and was getting home later and later from wherever it was he was going. I remember saying to my husband that maybe he was up to no good."

"What made you think that?"

Nina shuffled forward on her seat. "There was this one evening where he came down from his room, as white as a sheet. He had this little cloth bag in his hands. And he said, 'I've got a bit of business to take care of, but if anything happens to me, these are for my family. I'm going to put them somewhere safe.' He waved the bag at us, but we didn't have any idea what he was talking about."

My heart leaped. The forget-me-not diamonds!

"Did he say where he was putting the bag?"

Nina thought about it and shook her head. "No. He was rambling a bit. But he said he was going to leave an important message in… Now what was it? Something about a month." Old Nina's forehead scrunched up as she thought. Then she slapped her palm on the table. "March! That was it. He said he was going to let his family know that there would be a message in March. He was acting very strangely and I think he was just telling us to reassure himself about what he was doing."

"What does March mean?" I asked. "Did something happen in March?"

Nina shrugged. "No. This was in October and by the time March came, he'd disappeared and I had forgotten all about it. No one from his family turned up, so I assume the message never reached them. I think, looking back, it sounded like he knew someone was on his tail and was, well, frightened, I suppose. Like I said, he didn't pay his bill and we think he stole from us. We were pleased he'd gone, to be honest."

March. What did that mean? I couldn't wait to tell Matthew and Melody.

"Now, Jake, that's enough about me," said Nina. "What are we going to do about your mum?" She glanced at the mess.

"What do you mean? Everything is fine," I said.

"I'll have a chat with Michael when we get home. Maybe he can help us have a little clear-up here?" she said, pushing herself up to standing. "He's been doing a wonderful job at the Rectory."

"Ripping your house to bits isn't helping," I muttered, quietly.

"What was that, Jake?" said Nina.

"I don't want Michael's help," I snapped.

Nina flinched. "Why do you say that?"

I shrugged and paused. "Has he been kind to you, Nina?"

She frowned, puzzled by my question, but then she smiled. "It's been wonderful having him home again,

Jake," she said. "And meeting a grandson I never knew I had is the icing on the cake."

I swallowed the lump in my throat. I couldn't say anything else about Michael. Not now. We needed more proof.

"Right, I must get over to Mr Charles's. It was so nice of him to invite us and I've not even made an appearance yet!" she said.

After she'd left I ran upstairs to see how Mum was, hoping she wasn't going to start saying strange things again. She was asleep, curled up on her side. For a second I thought about lying next to her and putting an arm over hers. I usually pushed her away if she tried to hug me, but I wouldn't have done that now. I watched as her eyelids flickered, and I wondered if she was having a nice dream or a nightmare about people watching from outside? I closed the door quietly and made my way downstairs. I sat on the bottom step. Wilson came over, his tail wagging, and he sat close, nestled beside my leg. It was nice feeling his warm body beside me.

"What are we going to do, Wilson?" I said, stroking his head. "What are we going to do?"

Chapter 28

Rubble and Mix

We arranged to meet the following morning to discuss everything that had happened at Mr Charles's and what I'd learned from Old Nina. Matthew was already on to the next part of the investigation.

> MATTHEW: I've been doing some research online. Rubble and Mix used to have an office on the Trojan Industrial Estate. Shall we go and have a look? *If* it's still there.
>
> MELODY: Definitely. Let's meet at 10.

JAKE: Great. And I've got some news about Preston that Nina told me. I'll tell you all about it then.

MELODY: EEEK!

I got out of bed and put on yesterday's clothes and found a clean jumper in the bottom of my wardrobe. There was a noise outside and I looked round my curtain. The door of the Rectory opened and Michael appeared, carrying the tailor's dummy that Melody and I had seen in the dark cellar under his arm. Danny followed with a battered wooden box. He must be turning his attentions to the cellar. The pile on the front garden had grown and there was now an old dark-brown bookcase with a split in its side standing on top of the old rugs and pieces of carpet. Balancing on top, like a dusty star on a Christmas tree, was the old yellowing chandelier. I watched as they went back inside, presumably to get more stuff. It was horrible to see him wrecking her house. That was Old Nina's home! How dare he pull it to pieces! It made me more determined than ever. We *had* to find those diamonds first.

I poked my head round Mum's door. She was

sitting with her arms wrapped round her knees and she was rocking a little back and forth.

"Hi, Mum. Would you like anything?" I said, trying to sound bright and like everything was completely normal.

She wiped at her hair. It was greasy and sticking to her forehead. "Oh, good. You're here. I thought they'd taken you and you'd left me as well," she said.

I sat on her bed, beside her. "There isn't anyone, Mum. OK? I told you yesterday. It's only two days until you see the doctor. OK?"

She nodded, her eyes watery, and started nibbling the tops of her nails.

I made some toast, then delivered it to Mum with a tea, but she had gone back to sleep. I sighed, leaving the mug and plate on her bedside cabinet with all the other uneaten food I'd left there. I never knew anyone could sleep more than they were awake. I really hoped the doctor would be able to help.

The Trojan Industrial Estate was on the outskirts of town. It was a long walk and, on the way, I told them my theory.

"Did you see Michael has cleared out more stuff?" said Matthew.

"Yes. But I think he's desperate, don't you?" said Melody. "If he is looking for the diamonds, he doesn't have a clue where they are."

I kicked a stone as we walked. "If he carries on like this, there'll be nothing left of the Rectory."

Melody filled me in on what had happened at Mr Charles's house.

"It was almost like Mr Charles was playing a part he didn't realize he had!" She laughed. "He was acting like a real showman, showing off his plants and feeding the fish so that Danny could watch them come to the surface. We were there for ages."

"And how was Michael? Any suspicious behaviour?"

"Not really," said Matthew. "But he kept looking over at your house, Jake. It was like he was worried about you talking to Nina. Maybe he thinks we are on to something."

"Yes. He asked us what we were up to today and if Danny could come along but we said we weren't doing anything," said Melody.

"That's good," I said, then checked behind us, just to make sure that Michael or Danny weren't following.

"So, come on, Jake. What did Nina say?" said Melody.

We crossed over a busy road and I told them how I'd explained Piers and Preston were the same man and that Old Nina had said that she'd got herself in a worry about looking guilty if she took the suitcase to the police. "And she said something important," I said, grinning. "Something huge, in fact! I think she saw Preston with the *actual* bag of diamonds!"

"What? How? When?" said Melody excitedly. "Does she know where he hid them?"

"I'll explain everything if you give me a chance, Melody!"

Melody smiled. "Sorry. Carry on."

I told them what Preston had said to Nina – about there being a message in March.

"A message about what and to who?" said Matthew.

"About the diamonds to his family, I guess. Remember Tina said Preston told Jed that his family will know where to find them. He must have been intending to get a message to them somehow. Maybe in March," I said.

"It might have been a phone call," said Matthew.

"Or a letter, telling them where the diamonds were hidden," said Melody.

This was hard. The message was so cryptic.

"If there was a phone call or a letter in March, that

was years ago now," I said. "We'll never know what happened to the diamonds."

We carried on walking and passed a row of boarded-up shops and the main town car park. Before long we came to the entrance to the Trojan Industrial Estate. On the side of the road was a large sign with a list of businesses on the estate and a map showing where to find them.

Melody ran her finger down the list. "There's no Rubble and Mix listed," she said.

Matthew looked at something on his phone. "According to what I found, the address they used was Unit Seven," he said.

"There's bound to be another company using that unit now, though, isn't there?" I said.

"It's worth checking," said Melody.

I studied the map and tapped my finger on a purple-shaped square that was tucked in a corner. "Here it is. Unit Seven."

We entered the industrial estate. There were a few businesses that seemed to be open and I read the signs as we passed – a window manufacturer, a printing firm and a place that made dentures – but a lot of the units seemed to be either empty or the shutters were pulled down. We passed a man taking some paint pots out of the back of a van and a delivery driver carrying a large box, but no one took any notice of us.

"Unit Seven must be over there," I said, pointing to a row of four. Each of the single-storey buildings had a large window and door at the front. I looked in and they all appeared to be full of junk and as if they had not been used for some time. Unit Seven had its blinds closed and the door was padlocked.

"Look! It still says 'Rubble and Mix Ltd'," said Matthew, pointing to a small notice in the corner of the window that had faded from many years in the sun. Along the windowsill were dozens of dead flies, their legs in the air.

Melody cupped her hands round her eyes and tried to see in through any gaps in the blinds. "I can't see anything; it's too dark," she said. She rattled the padlock on the door. "Maybe we can pick this somehow?"

"We'll get in trouble for breaking and entering if we do that," said Matthew.

I remembered something. "We won't be breaking in if we have the key," I said. "Hang on a minute."

I shook the sports kit bag off my shoulders – the one I carried my EpiPen in – and opened it, feeling around inside. "Remember this from the toiletry bag in the suitcase?" I said, taking out the small silver key.

"Oh yes!" said Matthew.

I picked up the lock and put the key in, giving it a little wiggle. "I don't think it's been unlocked for years," I said. "Or maybe this isn't the right key." But then it clicked and popped open. I unhooked the padlock and pushed on the door. It was hard to move and I realized there was a large pile of letters, flyers, newspapers and magazines creating a huge mound behind the door. I shoved harder and the door swept them to one side. "No one has been in here for a while."

Melody closed the door behind us. There was a bolt on the inside and she pulled it across. "Just in case we're disturbed," she said, a sparkle of excitement in her eyes.

It was dark and Melody pulled on a cord at the side of the blinds and the slats eased open slightly. Dust particles danced in the light as we took in our surroundings.

"There's the evidence that someone has already been here looking for the diamonds," said Matthew. "Look!"

Along one side of the office were some old

metal filing cabinets. Most of the drawers had been pulled open and there were papers and files strewn everywhere. In the middle of the room were two desks facing each other, with large computers taking up much of the space. There were some upturned drawers on the desks that were littered with paperclips, pens, staplers, a large hole punch and more paperwork. One desk had a black swivel chair beside it, and I took a seat.

"Wow. Look at the computers! They're prehistoric," I said. I ran my finger across the screen taking off a thick layer of dust.

There was an old grey telephone on one of the desks and Melody picked up the receiver, which was attached with a curly lead, and put it to her ear. "It's dead," she said. "It must be disconnected." She placed it back with a clunk.

"What do you think this is?" said Matthew, standing by a machine that was resting on a low cabinet. "It's too small to be a photocopier."

Melody went over. "That's a fax machine. My dad told me about those. They used to use them to send documents to each other years ago. You put a piece of paper in one end, dial a number and it comes out of someone else's fax machine anywhere in the world."

Matthew nodded. "Cool," he said.

"Right, everyone, look around," said Melody.

"It would be easier if we knew exactly what we were looking for," I said. "Where do we start?"

Matthew studied a large red-and-white wall planner that was pinned above the fax machine. He read out some of the handwritten notes that were dotted on the weeks.

"*Groundwork starts at fifty-two Elm Road*; *Order floor tiles*; *Plumbers.* Boring!"

"Hang on," I said, stepping forward. "Is there a message for Preston's family written in March?"

"Great idea, Jake," said Melody.

I ran my finger along the columns that covered March but there were only notes about suppliers and foundations. Nothing that sounded like a clue or message.

"Let's check the cabinets," said Melody. She pulled on a metal drawer that hadn't been fully opened. It creaked and scraped. Inside were rows of cardboard pockets with little tabs on them.

"These are in month order," said Melody.

"Look for a file for March!" I said.

Melody scrambled her fingers through the files, then pushed it closed. "Nothing," she said.

Most of the drawers had been upturned so I searched around among the files on the floor. The room darkened a little as a shadow went past the window. We all froze and looked towards the door. The handle slowly pushed downwards. Someone was trying to get in!

"Get down!" whispered Matthew. The three of us ducked and I squeezed myself under the desk, looking towards the window.

A face appeared and a hand cupped round the eyes and against the glass as they peered in. It was hard to see who it was through the slats, but I knew it was someone short with dark hair. Was it Danny? The door handle rattled a few more times, and then a shadow went past the window the way they'd come.

We slowly crept out of our hiding places.

"That was Danny! I'm sure of it," I said. "He must have followed us, trying to see what we were up to."

"Well, he's gone for now," said Matthew. "Let's keep looking."

I moved a few files around on the floor – January, December, July and then, there it was. "March! I've found it," I said.

We put the file on the desk and opened it up. Inside were lots of pieces of paper, including a large, folded sheet. It was huge and we had to move some of the clutter out of the way so we could open it fully.

"I think it's an architect's plans," said Matthew. "It looks like Rubble and Mix were building some new houses. Next to one that was already built by the looks of it." He pointed at the pencilled words written underneath a drawing of an older house. "*The Rectory*," he read.

We stared at the plans and then the reality hit us.

"That's our road!" I said. "That's Chestnut Close!"

Chapter 29

A New Clue

"Rubble and Mix built our houses!" said Melody.

We huddled together to take a closer look at the drawings.

"That's my house!" I said. "Look, it says number five and number seven." I moved my finger round the edge of the semi-circle. "That's Matthew's and Mr Charles's. And there is number one and yours too, Melody."

I looked through the rest of the papers that were in the file. One was a letter to the council's planning department and it was signed. "It's him! It's Preston James! They started building our homes in March 1997."

"Hold on, there's something written by the Rectory," said Matthew. He tapped his finger and squinted. In small black handwriting were some letters:

$$EIQFRTSOTK$$

"What does that mean?" said Melody. "Is it an anagram?"

"No, it can't be," I said. "There's a 'Q' and no 'U'."

None of the other houses had anything written beside them. Matthew turned the file over. I searched the rest of the file and at the back, in the cardboard wallet that kept everything together, was a flap, almost hidden.

"There's a little pocket here!" I said. I put my fingers in and pulled out a small white envelope. On the front it read:

For Leonard

"Who's Leonard?" said Melody.

Matthew shook his head and shrugged.

I ripped open the envelope. It was a handwritten letter. I flattened the piece of paper and began to read. *"Dear Leonard. If you are reading this, then my message about March has reached you."* I looked up at my friends. "This letter must be from Preston! But the message didn't reach him, did it? March wasn't about a phone call or a letter; he wanted to tell his family to look in the March *file*. Whoever searched the office didn't have that clue where to look – that's why the letter is still here. They never found it!"

"Keep going, Jake," said Matthew, trying to read it over my shoulder.

"Well done, son. I am proud of you. You will be a worthy successor to the business. The notebook with the addresses of the houses we've been working on – the ones with the 'special' latches and locks – is hidden in the safe. You know the code."

We looked around the office for signs of a safe.

"It's here under the desk!" said Matthew. "It's open and empty so whoever ransacked the office must have taken the book of addresses."

I went back to the letter. *"I'm sorry I had to send you and your mum away. Things are hotting up with Jed and I don't want to put you in danger. I also have to make sure your granddad is sorted before I leave, as I won't be around to help him. I'm just waiting for some cash to come through on a deal, and then I can leave him with enough money to live out the rest of his days. When that's done, I'll be on my way. It'll be worth it, I promise!"*

"That's why he didn't run off with his wife and son, then," said Melody. "Keep going, Jake."

"*I'm staying in a room with this dopey couple on a street where we built some houses a couple of years ago.* He's talking about Old Nina and her husband!" I said. "What a cheek."

I carried on. "*I'll be home as soon as everything is done, but just in case anything happens to me I have left you a message on the plans saying exactly where to find the 'package'. Remember our secret code? I believe in you, son. When you find them you and your mum will be sorted for life. There's over a million there at least. Love, Dad.*" I looked up at the others.

"The package he's talking about must be the diamonds!" said Melody.

"But the letter never got to Leonard, so the forget-me-not diamonds must still be there! The diamonds are hidden in the Rectory!" said Matthew.

"Right. Focus! Let's have another look at that code," said Melody.

We studied the strange letters again and Melody took a sheet of paper from the top of an old photocopier and wrote them down.

"Anyone got any ideas?" I asked.

Matthew was trying a few things on his phone, but he shook his head. "No luck."

"Who is the cleverest person we know?" said Melody. "We need to find someone who will take one look at this and know instantly what it means."

I frowned as I thought about it. And then Melody and I stared straight at each other and smiled as we realized we were both thinking of the same person.

"Brian!" we both said.

"Yes, we should ask your dad, Matthew!" I said.

Matthew frowned. "Oh, what? Why him?"

"He'd be perfect!" said Melody. "Your dad knows *everything*, Matthew. You can ask him who was on the throne in 1782 and he knows the answer. He's amazing! He'll solve this in seconds."

Matthew huffed. He did not look happy.

"Come on, Matthew. He hasn't won all those quizzes with Brian's Brains for nothing," I said.

Matthew rubbed the side of his face. "He'll not stop going on about it if we get him involved. *And* he'll want to know what we're up to."

Melody folded the sheet of paper and put it in the pocket of her jeans. "We don't need to tell him what it's for. We just say the usual thing we say when we don't want someone to know why we're asking," she said.

"It's for homework!" the three of us said in unison, and we all burst out laughing. For a second I felt like the luckiest person alive. I had the nicest friends in the world, even though I hadn't always been the nicest to them in the past.

"Where's your dad now, Matthew?" Melody asked.

Matthew checked the time on his phone. "He works from home on Tuesdays, but it's lunchtime so he'll be in the Magpie pub meeting the rest of Brian's Brains."

"Is there a quiz today then?" said Melody.

"No. They meet once a week so they can test each other's knowledge. It's well sad."

"This is brilliant," I said. "We are going to meet the award-winning Brian's Brains at last!"

Matthew sighed, his shoulders dropping. "Terrific."

"Come on, then," said Melody. "Let's go!"

Chapter 30

Brian's Brains

As we hurried back to the high street, Matthew gave us instructions on how to talk to his dad, even though we've both known him for years.

"Just ask him about the code, get the answer and leave. Whatever you do, don't ask him or any of the team anything about quizzing or their favourite topics or anything related to questions, cryptic clues, that kind of thing. If you do we'll never get away. Trust me."

Melody kept giggling and I must admit it was funny when Matthew was like this. Melody and I both thought Brian was great, but I guess Matthew saw him differently being his son.

We reached the Magpie pub and I put my hand on the door. "Are we allowed in here?" I asked.

"Yeah, we can go to the lounge bit where they'll be sitting. Just don't go near the bar," said Matthew.

Inside, the pub was deserted, apart from a woman wearing thick-rimmed glasses, wiping the dark brown bar with a grey tea towel. She glanced up at us and carried on wiping.

Matthew marched towards a room that was tucked round the side, which had the word 'LOUNGE' written above the doorway. 'Lounge' was a bit of an exaggeration, as it was just a cold square room with two wooden tables surrounded by an assortment of chairs. One table was occupied and was piled high with books, notepads, a kitchen timer in the shape of a boiled egg, pencils and four glasses of cola. Brian was sitting at the head of the table and hadn't noticed us as he was busy scrolling on his phone. Beside him was a woman with long grey hair wearing a pale pink beret, who was bent over one of the books, running her finger down the index. The other two members were having a heated debate.

"It was 1657! Honestly, Margaret. I thought history was your best subject," said a man wearing a denim shirt over a navy-blue T-shirt. He laughed and shook his head at Margaret, who glared at him as she removed her glasses and began to polish them with a silver scarf that was draped round her shoulders.

"It was 1658, Himesh. Oliver Cromwell died in 1658. How you can possibly think it was fifty-seven is beyond me."

Himesh looked over at Brian. "Anything?" he asked.

Brian shook his head. "I can't get on the Wi-Fi."

The woman who was looking in the index of the book suddenly exclaimed. "Aha! I've got it. Here we go!"

Margaret put her glasses back on. "Go on, Teresa. Put Himesh out of his misery."

Teresa turned the heavy book to the beginning and flicked through the pages. "Who needs the internet when you can use a good old-fashioned book?" she muttered.

"You are going down, Margaret!" said Himesh, pointing a finger at the woman who pulled an amused face back at him. "1657 all day long!"

Brian, Himesh and Margaret began to smack the palms of their hands on the table in a rumble that increased in volume, building the tension.

"Crikey. They really are … serious," whispered Melody.

"Yep. See what I mean?" said Matthew with a sigh.

Teresa cleared her throat and the slapping hands stopped abruptly, Himesh shhhing everyone even though no one had spoken.

"Oliver Cromwell," said Teresa in a clear voice, "died on the third of September in sixteen ... fifty-eight! Ten points to Margaret!"

"Oh, what?" said Himesh, slumping in his seat.

"YES! Get in," said Margaret.

Brian suddenly spotted the three of us standing in the doorway. "Matthew! What are you doing here?" He waved his hand at us. "Everyone? You know my son, Matthew, and these are our neighbours Melody and Jake."

There was a sudden look of panic on Brian's face and he quickly checked his watch. "Your mum hasn't told you to get me, has she? There's no signal in here."

"No, Dad," said Matthew.

"We've actually come to ask for help with solving something," said Melody.

Himesh sat bolt upright. "What needs solving? Pray tell," he asked.

Melody took the folded sheet of paper from her pocket and placed it in the centre of the table. Brian's Brains collectively leaned over.

"What's this, then?" asked Margaret.

"It's a coded message, of course," said Himesh. He looked up at us. "And you want us to tell you what it says?"

"Please," said Matthew.

Brian, Margaret and Teresa had already taken up notepads and were copying down the letters and scribbling other letters, and some numbers, beside them. They were clearly trying to race to see who could get the answer the quickest.

Matthew looked at me and Melody, raising his eyebrows. The table had fallen silent and there was a lot of sighing and crossing things out. After a few more minutes, Brian sat back and threw his pen on to the table with a clatter. "I've got it," he said, smiling.

"You haven't," said Teresa. "Not that quickly, surely."

Brian took a sip of his cola and shrugged. He looked so pleased with himself. Margaret clicked her pen and closed her notepad. "Go on then, Brian. Tell us," she said.

Brian picked his pen up and smiled at his teammates. "You're going to kick yourselves. It's an easy one!"

Himesh frowned, then a big grin spread across his face too. "Oh, I see it now. It's good old QWERTY!"

"QWERTY?" I said. "What's that mean?"

"I'll show you," said Brian. He ripped out a blank page from his notepad and turned it on its side then began to write out the alphabet.

ABCDEFGHIJKLMNOPQRSTUVWXYZ

Beneath it, he wrote another series of letters. They all looked a bit random to me.

QWERTYUIOPASDFGHJKLZXCVBNM

"What are you doing?" said Melody.

"It's an old classic code where you line up the alphabet with the QWERTY keyboard."

"What's a QWERTY keyboard?" said Matthew.

Teresa picked up a bag from the floor, took out a laptop and flipped it open. "It's the name for the way the alphabet is arranged on computers, laptops, old typewriters, that kind of thing. See?" She pointed to the top row of letters. "It reads as 'QWERTY'. It never reads as A, B, C. It's been set out like that for decades. And now Brian has broken the code we can work out what it says."

Brian turned back to his piece of paper and circled

the letters that corresponded to the letters of the coded message, writing each one beneath it.

A B C D E F G H I J K L M N O P Q R S T U V W X Y Z
Q W E R T Y U I O P A S D F G H J R L Z X C V B N M

E I Q F R T S O T K
C H A N D E L I E R

"Oh. My. Goodness," said Melody.

"That's it! That's where he hid them!" I said.

"Shhh!! Jake!" said Matthew.

I clamped my hand over my mouth.

The four members of Brian's Brains were silent and staring at us.

"Where who hid what?" said Margaret slowly.

"Yes, you three, what is going on here?" said Brian. "Why are you trying to break this code? What's it for?"

We looked at each other. Then: "It's for homework!" we all shouted.

Melody grabbed the sheet of paper from Brian, and with a loud "Thanks, Brian's Brains!" from me and a cheesy thumbs up from Matthew, we ran out of the pub.

Chapter 31

Right Under Our Noses

"The diamonds are hidden in the chandelier!" I said as we hurried along the road. "Michael must have removed it to look in the ceiling and it's been in the front garden all this time."

"I don't believe it!" said Matthew.

"There must be millions of pounds just sitting on top of a pile of rubbish," said Melody, out of breath.

We hurried on and Matthew glanced behind him. "Don't look round, but I think we're being followed."

Melody couldn't help herself and turned round. "That's Michael's car!" she said.

"Or is it Preston's son Leonard?" I said. Everything

was falling into place now. "Don't you think that makes more sense? Leonard is pretending to be Michael! It was *his* dad's skeleton found in Nina's back garden. He saw it on the news then did some snooping on Nina, found out from some old article that she'd lost a son called Michael when they were on holiday and BAM! That was his way in! He's here to find out where his dad hid the diamonds!"

"I feel sick," said Matthew. I wasn't sure if that was from hearing my theory about Leonard, or because of how fast we were walking.

"I think you're right," said Melody. "There was that hankie in his jacket too with his initials – 'L. J'."

"Let's go this way and try and lose him," I said. I knew a lot of the side roads from cycling. I turned left and then we crossed over and turned right. I checked behind us and saw the black car indicating to turn into the street we were heading down.

"We are definitely being followed," I said. "Danny is in the front. I told you it was him at the office, trying to get in. He must have told his dad and they followed us to the pub. They know we're on to something."

We took a few more turns and then ended up back on the high street and ducked into a bookshop. We watched out of the window as the car crawled past in a line of slow-moving traffic. There was no place for Michael to pull over and we watched as the black car disappeared beyond the traffic lights.

"He's gone," I said, letting out a sigh.

"Maybe now is the time to call the police?" said Matthew. "We can tell them about Jed and how Michael is a fraud."

"And let them find the forget-me-not diamonds and take the glory? No way," said Melody. "We are so close! We can call them when we've got the diamonds in our hands."

Melody picked up a blue-and-orange book from a display and read the blurb, chewing on her cheek.

"Melody! Come on, this is not a good time for reading," I said.

"Any time is a good time for reading, Jake," she said.

I rolled my eyes as she put the book back.

"Why don't we just go home and act casual?" said Matthew. "We don't need to let on about anything. We can get the chandelier after dark or even tomorrow. It's not going anywhere!"

"Apart from the tip to be crushed to dust if it hasn't been already," I said.

Matthew shook his head. "I guess it is a bit risky just leaving it there," he said.

"We have to get it as soon as possible," I said.

"Agreed," said Melody. "But I'm just going to buy this first." She took the blue-and-orange book from the shelf again and quickly trotted to the desk.

As we walked along Chestnut Close we saw Michael's car parked outside the Rectory.

"They're probably watching from the window, so everyone just act natural," I said through the side of my mouth. We reached the NOW LET sign outside number one and stopped. Melody tipped her head back and let out a loud laugh.

"Melody!" snapped Matthew. "What are you doing?"

"I'm acting natural!" said Melody. "You've just said something funny, Jake. Let's all laugh!"

Matthew raised his eyebrows at me but we both managed to chuckle about a non-existent joke.

"See? We're being normal; we are just acting very, very cool," she said.

"Then stop looking over at the house!" I said sharply. Her eyes kept darting to the Rectory. I couldn't resist a look myself. Was it still there? Behind the front hedge I could see the top of the dark brown bookcase. And there was the chandelier, half hanging off.

Matthew gasped. "I don't want to worry anyone, but Danny is coming."

"Whatever you do, don't mention the diamonds!" said Melody.

I saw Danny's eyes widen a little. Had he heard her?

"Hi!" he said. He was working at his puzzle box at breakneck speed and I wondered if he played with it more when he was anxious.

"Oh, hi, Danny!" said Melody. "How are you today?"

I groaned inwardly. She sounded so fake!

"Um. I'm all right," said Danny, standing before us. "Where have you been? Anywhere nice?"

We all answered in unison.

"Shopping."

"Bowling."

"Library."

Danny frowned. "Wow. That's a lot of things. You've been busy."

I nodded. "Yep. We have," I said. "Anyway. We have to get going, don't we, Matthew?"

Matthew flushed. Lying made him uncomfortable. "Um. Yes, yes, we do," he said.

Danny was staring at Melody and I noticed her gaze kept being drawn across the close to the Rectory. I gave her a nudge and she snapped out of it.

"Are we going to try and find the diamonds then?" said Danny, his fingers still fidgeting with the puzzle box.

Matthew let out a cough and Melody chewed her lip, her eyes darting behind his shoulder.

"Oh, we're not doing that any more," I said.

"Yes. Tina was just showing off," said Matthew. "It was all made up."

"Really?" said Danny. "That seems odd to just give up like that when you were so keen before."

I shrugged. "Shall we go?" I said to Matthew and Melody.

But Danny stood in our way.

"Are you sure it isn't because you've already found them?" He dropped his arms and stepped closer to Melody. "What were you looking at just then, Melody?"

He turned and followed her gaze and his hands dropped by his sides. Just then the sun came out from behind a cloud. The light seemed to catch the top of the chandelier and the glass droplets twinkled. I was just wondering which ones might be the diamonds when Danny gasped and sprinted back to the Rectory.

He knew exactly where they were.

Chapter 32

A Tug of War

Danny ran to the chandelier and attempted to pick it up, but it was far too big and heavy. He gave up and pounded on the door of the Rectory, looking back to check on us every few thumps.

"We've got to get it NOW!" I said. We followed Danny to the pile outside the Rectory. We each grabbed hold of the chandelier and carried it to the pavement. It tinkled as it moved and a few droplets came loose and smashed on to the ground into tiny pieces.

"Don't break it!" said Matthew.

"Diamonds won't smash. They're too hard," I said,

remembering an old science lesson. "It's just the glass bits that are smashing."

The door of the Rectory opened and we hesitated about which direction to go in. Michael's large figure was suddenly pacing towards us, Danny hurrying behind.

"Hey there!" said Michael, still putting on his friendly face. "I'm afraid I need to take that. Mum wants me to put it back up. I can't quite get her to part with the old stuff just yet!" He laughed and reached a hand towards the chandelier.

"Um. No. I don't think so," I said.

Danny stepped out from behind his dad. "Dad's right. Granny wants it back," he said. For a moment I thought maybe we had everything wrong. Maybe this man and his son really *were* related to Nina and were just thinking of her. But then I saw Danny's furrowed forehead. He looked scared.

"Danny?" I said. "Are you OK?"

Danny shuffled up beside me and put his hand up by his mouth to whisper. "You should hand it over," he said quietly. "Dad doesn't like it when he doesn't get his way."

His dad must have heard, because he took a step closer, the friendly smile gone.

"Danny is right. You should hand it over before you regret it." He took another step towards us and we stepped back. Matthew caught his foot on the edge of the kerb and stumbled, letting go. Danny was nearest to us and his dad shouted, "Grab it, son!" and Danny reached out and took hold of it where Matthew had been.

"I've got it, Dad! I've got it!" said Danny. But he seemed more scared about it than happy.

Melody and I were still holding on but she was looking at me wide-eyed. Had we taken on too much here? Maybe we *should* have called the police.

"Enough of these ridiculous games!" bellowed Michael. "Let go NOW!"

Danny tugged the chandelier but Melody and I pulled it back and he let go, running to be beside his dad who shook his head despairingly.

Matthew took hold of it again.

"There is no way we are giving this to you, so just give up, Michael," I said. "Or should I say … Leonard!"

Danny gasped and put his hand over his mouth. There was silence as we waited for Michael/Leonard to say something. Was he going to deny it? Another piece of glass fell and smashed.

"Dad?" said Danny. "You said no one would know who you were!"

"Shut it, Danny!"

Danny flinched at his dad's words and his head drooped as he put his hands in the pocket of his hoodie.

"You aren't Michael, are you? You've been lying to everyone," said Melody. The curtain of the Rectory moved and I saw Old Nina looking out. All I wanted in that moment was for him to say no, that he was Michael, that he truly was Nina's long-lost son.

"Who are you really?" said Matthew.

The man claiming to be Old Nina's son sighed and shrugged as if this question was a mere inconvenience to him.

"Does it matter?" he said, huffing. He rolled his eyes. "OK. Yes, I'm Leonard. My father was Preston James. So what?"

I felt tears prickle the backs of my eyes. "You lied!" I said. "You pretended to be Nina's dead son. How could you be so cruel?"

He laughed, then rubbed his hand over his stubbled chin. "She'll get over it, the daft bat. Now, if I'm correct, I think you three have done the hard work for me and found the diamonds. So, that there" – he pointed to the chandelier – "rightly belongs to me." He lurched forward and grabbed a side. "Come on. Don't be silly," he said, tugging the chandelier towards him. He was strong and we jerked against the force of his pull.

"Don't let go," I said to my friends. "We can win this."

"Ha, really?" said Leonard, yanking it towards himself again. Matthew's hands slipped and he lost his grip again.

Out of the corner of my eye I saw Danny take his mobile phone out of his pocket and press the screen. This was worrying. Was he calling for backup from their gangster friends?

The door to the Rectory opened. My heart sank. Nina. I didn't want her to witness this.

"Go back inside, Nina!" I called through gritted teeth.

But Nina walked down her pathway.

"Michael? Is everything OK?" she said, her voice thin.

Leonard looked across at her, a big, forced smile returning to his face. "Everything is absolutely fine, *Mum*!" he called, emphasizing the word and raising his eyebrows at me. "Danny, give me a hand, eh?"

Danny had started to cry. The phone was still gripped tightly in his hand. But he didn't make any move to help.

"Dad, stop it! Please stop. That's enough," he said. "You are Leonard James and you are causing a … a disturbance on … on Chestnut Close! Hurry!"

Leonard looked puzzled. "Hurry? Why are you talking like that, Danny?" he said. "I'm doing this for you, son. Now grab hold!"

Danny shook his head.

"You are part of this!" shouted Leonard. "You were so clever, son. You followed them to the office and then to that pub. You let me know what was going on. You've been brilliant! We've nearly done it, haven't we?"

I saw Nina put a hand to her open mouth.

Danny was shaking. "But … but I didn't … want to do anything. I only did it because it made you happy. These are nice people, Dad. They're my friends."

The door to number seven opened and Kyle and Cameron came out. Leonard jerked his head around, checking if anyone else was coming. He was slowly being surrounded by our neighbours.

"What's all this about?" said Cameron.

Kyle had his bassoon strung round his neck and he held it like it was a weapon.

"This isn't Michael!" I said. "His name is Leonard James and he's been pretending to be Nina's son so he can try and find some diamonds."

"Do we need to call the police?" said Kyle.

In the distance I heard the sound of a siren.

"Someone already has," said Danny between sobs.

I looked down at his phone that was lit up in his hand. He'd called the police and let them hear the rest. That's why he'd said our address out loud.

"I'm sorry, Dad. But you have to stop! You can't do this any more!"

Leonard closed his eyes for a second and gave a slight shake of his head. "Danny, I'm doing this for *you*."

"No, you're not! You're doing it for yourself! You're trying to be a big mean man like your father was. But you're not. You're not mean! You're not like this!"

Nina was standing with us now and Danny threw his arms round her, sobbing. "I'm sorry," he said. "I'm sorry we lied."

Nina tilted her chin upwards, a calm but stern look on her face as she stared at Leonard.

"You are not my son, are you?" she said.

For a second Leonard looked almost embarrassed and I wondered if the magnitude of the pain he was about to cause had suddenly hit him.

"No," he said. He dropped his chin slightly. "I saw your house on the news when Dad's body was found and looked you up. I found out about Michael and decided that your long-lost son was my way in."

"But … why?" said Nina.

Leonard shrugged. "For the diamonds, of course. I knew Dad would have stashed them somewhere safe to stop Jed getting his hands on them. And I was right about that, wasn't I?" He glared at us and gave the chandelier another tug.

The police sirens were closer now. Cameron stepped forward and gave Leonard a shove. "You've done enough damage," he said. "Just give it up."

Leonard glared at him, and then his hand dropped as he let go. He looked up at the blue flashing lights turning into our road, then he ran, straight down the alleyway and into the graveyard.

"DAD!" called Danny.

Nina patted him on his back and stroked his hair.

"It's OK," she said, as the tears streamed down her face. "Everything is going to be OK."

Chapter 33

A Tumbling World

The police car screeched to a halt outside Mr Charles's house and four officers got out. Mr Charles hurried down his pathway and Kyle went over to fill him in. Melody and I carefully put the chandelier down on the ground.

One of the police officers walked over to us. "Everyone all right here?" he said. "We had a call saying a Leonard James is in the vicinity and causing a disturbance."

"He went that way!" I said, pointing to the alley.

Three of the officers ran towards the graveyard

and the one who stayed behind called on his radio for backup.

The policeman turned to us. "We've been looking for Mr James for a few years. He's been on our radar for repeated breaking and entering. And since finding his dad, we thought he might resurface trying to find his old man's hoard. He and his business partner were linked to a bunch of precious diamonds that have been missing for years. The forget-me-not diamonds."

I cleared my throat. "I think we've found them actually," I said. I nodded to the chandelier.

"Really?" said the policeman, frowning. "In that thing?"

"The forget-me-not diamonds are hidden in it," said Melody. "We solved a clue that Preston left and got to it before Leonard." It was then that I spotted a few of the droplets were different shapes to the rest and almost petal-like. They had a blue tinge to them. Were they the diamonds?

"It sounds like you've been busy," said the policeman.

Danny let go of Nina and stepped forward, his head held high. "Excuse me, officer? I'm Danny James. Leonard is my dad," he said. "What's going to happen to me?"

The policeman sighed. "I see. You'll have to stay here until someone comes to talk to you. We'll need to take statements from everyone here too."

"What about Nina?" said Kyle. "That man who ran off, whatever you said his name was, has been pretending to be her dead son."

We all looked at Nina then. She seemed almost hollow inside and the colour had drained from her cheeks. I reached out and held her hand, but it just hung limply in mine. Would she ever get over this?

"We'll get some more officers down here to speak to you too, Mrs Fennell," said the policeman. "Come on, Danny. Let's get you in the car and make a few calls, shall we?"

Danny dragged his feet as he walked and then he turned. "I wanted to tell you, I really did. But I didn't want to get him in trouble, you know?" He turned to Nina. "I'm sorry." He paused as his voice caught. "I wish you were my real grandma."

Nina had started to tremble. Cameron came and put his arm round her, but she just stared ahead blankly.

"Don't worry, Nina," I whispered. "We'll look after you." I moved out of the way, as Cameron and Kyle walked her back towards the Rectory. Mr Charles trotted ahead, opening her gate.

"It's going to be so painful for her," said Melody as we watched.

"Unbearable," said Matthew.

I swallowed the sob I could feel forming at the back of my throat.

"We'll just have to be the best neighbours to her that we can be," I said.

Just then my front door opened.

My heart sank. A woman I barely recognized stood in the doorway, greasy hair plastered to her head, dirty pink dressing gown tied tightly round her waist.

Mum.

"Is that ... Sue?" said Mr Charles. He turned to me. "Jake?"

I was frozen in panic. I didn't say anything. I couldn't. I didn't want this to happen. I didn't want everyone to see Mum like this. I knew she wouldn't want it either if she was feeling herself. She took a few steps down our driveway, her feet bare. She held up an arm and pointed towards the policeman who was with Danny by his car.

"You keep away from my son!" she said. The

policeman had his back to her and was talking on his radio and hadn't noticed her. Her eyes darted around wildly before her gaze found me. "Jake! Don't go with him!"

Matthew and Melody looked at me.

"Jake?" said Melody.

"What's going on?" Matthew said.

I shook my head. "It's … it's nothing," I said. "Mum, I'm fine! Go back inside. I'll be home in a minute!"

But Mum didn't move.

Just then, Claudia's car pulled on to her driveway and she hurried over. "What's going on?" she said. She looked at Mum and her jaw dropped a little. "Sue? Is everything OK?"

Mr Charles went to Mum and tried to put his arm round her, but she pushed him away.

"Jake," she said, her eyes shifting around at our neighbours as if they were strangers. "You need to come with me and we can get back inside and lock the door."

Claudia put her arms out as if trying to coax a frightened puppy. "Sue? It's me. Claudia. Shall we get you back inside? I can make us a nice cup of tea, yes?"

Mum ignored her and hurried towards me. I felt

like my world was tumbling downwards into a deep, dark hole. Why couldn't she have stayed inside where no one could see her? I caught Melody's eye and she shook her head ever so slightly. Matthew looked distraught.

Mum took a step closer and tried to put her arms round me but I wrestled myself free.

"What are you doing, Mum?" I said.

"I need to get you back where you'll be safe. I'm your mother and protecting you is my job," said Mum.

I took a step away. "You're not doing a very good job, are you? Look at you!" I waved my hand and Mum looked down at her tatty dressing gown, her dirty feet. She seemed to realize then how she must look and she put a hand to her face.

"I'm … I'm sorry," she said.

"Come on, Sue," said Claudia again.

This time Mum let Claudia put her arm round her shoulders and allowed herself to be gently guided back towards our house.

"Oh, Jake, why didn't you say something?" said Kyle.

"She made me promise not to tell anyone. I made her an appointment to see the doctor but I couldn't get her seen until Thursday. I hoped she'd be OK until then," I said, trying my hardest not to cry. "I was worried if I told anyone, I might not be able to stay with her." My voice was shaking.

"Your mum just needs the right kind of help," said Cameron. "And she probably needed to be seen quite urgently, I would have thought."

I watched as Mum headed through our front door with Claudia. Melody and Matthew stood beside me.

"Everything is going to be OK, Jake," said Melody softly.

"Yes, don't worry," said Matthew. "She'll be all right."

I wished I could believe that. What a mess. Nina and then Mum.

Mum would get help now, which was good, but things were probably going to change at home after everyone had seen how bad she was. And what would happen to me?

Chapter 34

Matthew's Secret

Claudia helped Mum to get showered and changed and settled her on the sofa, and then she rang the doctor and got her an emergency appointment for later in the day. I stood in the kitchen as she made a start on the mess.

"Things have been really hard for you, Jake, haven't they?" said Claudia as she lifted the piles of crockery out of the sink and turned on the hot tap. "You should have said something. We could have helped."

I kept quiet. If I spoke, I knew I'd start crying. I was so grateful that someone was helping me and I wouldn't have to be in charge any more. But I was scared too, for Mum and for me.

"Melody and Matthew are going to the shops to get you a few food bits," said Claudia. "When they get back, I suggest you go and have a walk with them and have a chat? I'll stay here with your mum and clear up a bit. And don't worry – me and Melody can stay here with you tonight."

I nodded and then dropped my head as the tears began to fall.

Melody and Matthew arrived an hour later with four bags of shopping, and Claudia told us to go off on our walk. I got Wilson ready, and Melody went home to get Frankie and we headed to the graveyard.

Nobody said anything to start with, and then Melody updated me with what had happened with Leonard. After everything with Mum, I'd almost forgotten he was on the run.

"They caught him in town trying to get on a train without a ticket," Melody said as we made our way down the alleyway.

"And what about Danny?" I said. "Is he OK?"

Melody shrugged. "We don't know. I guess we won't hear from him again."

Poor Danny. It wasn't his fault his dad was a

criminal, and the fact he'd called the police on him meant he must have had enough of that life.

We walked past the large horse chestnut tree and this time I bent down to pick up a shiny conker. I put it in my pocket. They were like the diamonds of a tree, I guess.

Matthew cleared his throat. "I'm sorry about your mum, Jake," he said. "You could have told us, you know?"

I shrugged. "Maybe," I said.

"We're friends, aren't we? We're here for each other, no matter what," he said.

I don't know why but I felt really angry with him for saying that.

"I know you mean well, Matthew, but you're good at keeping things to yourself too, you know?" I said.

"What do you mean?"

I took a breath. "Well, you have a secret too. You keep going somewhere and not telling us where. I saw you the other day. In Bargain Bonanza. You were buying cleaning products. Is your germ fear back again?"

Matthew looked puzzled. "No, I wasn't," he said, scowling.

"I saw you! And there was that girl on the bus. If

it's not your OCD, do you have other friends we don't know about?"

"No!" said Matthew. "And I wasn't buying cleaning stuff that day, actually. I was buying shoe polish if you must know."

"Shoe polish?" said Melody.

"Yes! I ... I've got a new hobby. I didn't say anything because, for a start, I might like to keep some parts of my life private, and also I thought you'd take the mickey."

He didn't say anything else.

"And?" I said.

Matthew frowned. "And what?"

"And what is your new hobby?" said Melody. "Come on, tell us."

Matthew huffed and rolled his eyes. "I've started dancing lessons. I'm doing all kinds. But mostly tap. That's how I knew the girl on the bus. We partner up for Latin sometimes."

"Is that it?" I said. I was so pleased that this was the reason and he wasn't going off with some new friends.

"Um, yes?" said Matthew.

"And the tapping you keep doing on your wrist?" I asked. "What's that all about?"

"If I'm feeling anxious, I practise the steps in my head. Tapping helps me to keep time, that's all."

I laughed. "That's just brilliant," I said. I guess you never really know everything about the people who are closest to you. Even if you think you do. And that is all right.

"I do struggle with my OCD," he said. "Every day feels like a battle and I'm trying my hardest not to go back to where I was."

"You can always talk to us. You know. When it's bad," I said.

Matthew didn't say anything.

"I think the dancing sounds really cool, Matthew," said Melody. "When can we come and see you in a show?"

"Er, let me think. Never?" said Matthew.

And we all laughed.

We walked for a bit in silence and when we got to Chestnut Close we went back to my house. Everything looked much cleaner already, and Mum was drinking a cup of tea on the sofa. She had changed into a jumper and jeans and she didn't look quite so pale. I thought Claudia must have helped brush her hair too, as it was tied back neatly. Matthew and Melody went out to the kitchen to give me some time with Mum on my own.

"Oh, Jake. I'm sorry," Mum said.

I felt a combination of sadness and embarrassment about what had happened in front of everyone. It proved that I was right – it was hard to keep a secret when you lived on Chestnut Close. But I was glad people knew the truth. My problem was shared now and my neighbours were going to help.

Claudia came into the lounge holding her mobile. "I've spoken to your Auntie Wendy, Jake," she said. She sat beside Mum and patted her hand. "Wendy said she's sorry. She shouldn't have taken the argument so seriously and she's always here for you. She said to tell you she loves you both very much indeed."

Mum let out a little sob and Claudia carried on. "She's getting the train tomorrow and said she'll stay at least two weeks."

That was the best news ever. I felt a wave of relief wash over me. Someone would be staying with us and helping!

"And I've talked to your boss, Sue. I've explained everything and he understands," Claudia continued.

I thought of Leo then. I would text him and ask if he could video-call me and I'd tell him everything. I thought it would be better that way.

I sat next to Mum and held her hand. Just seeing her a tiny bit brighter made me feel better.

"Shall we get going, Sue?" said Claudia.

Mum squeezed my fingers, and then they stood up and slowly made their way to Claudia's car.

After Mum and Claudia had gone, Melody and Matthew followed me to the hallway. I opened the door and saw the pile of furniture and pieces of carpet still in Nina's front garden.

"Maybe we could have some kind of rota to check in on Nina. She's going to find it extra hard now."

Melody nodded. "Yes. That's a good idea," she said.

"Mum and Dad will have her over for dinner now and then, I'm sure," said Matthew.

It wouldn't be the same as having Michael, but at least it was something.

We went to the front door and as we looked across at the Rectory there was a flicker in the window. Nina's lamp, guiding her son home, had been switched back on once more.

Chapter 35

The New Neighbours At Number One

Auntie Wendy arrived in a whirlwind of cooking, cleaning and lots and lots of talking. She'd been with us for ten days and I'd never known the house to be so noisy.

"You have been brilliant, Jake, keeping this house going all on your own," said Auntie Wendy one morning. She'd made me a bacon roll and I sat at the kitchen table eating it while she cleared up. Wilson stood at her feet, hoping something edible would be dropped. "Why didn't you call or text me? I would have been here in a heartbeat! Everything is going to be OK now, you know. Your mum's medication is working, and it won't be long until she has her first therapy session. Talking to someone will help her. She'll be back at work in no time. And the locksmiths are coming to all of the houses on the close tomorrow to check all the window and door latches. Are you going to walk that dog, then? He keeps sniffing around me!"

She looked at me, puzzled as to why I hadn't spoken yet, but not realizing I couldn't have got a word in edgeways if I'd tried.

I wiped tomato sauce from my mouth. "I'm walking him later with Melody and Matthew."

Auntie Wendy smiled and came over, ruffling my hair. "You're a good boy, Jake. I know it's been hard but I'm proud of you."

"Thanks."

She handed me a small plate with another bacon roll on it. "Can you give this to your mum for me?" Then she went to unload the washing machine.

Mum was in the garden sitting at our patio table with a mug of coffee in her hands. It was a cold, crisp day and the sky was a brilliant blue. Wilson followed me, trotting down the garden. Mum was all wrapped up in a coat and a scarf and she squinted up at me, smiling in the sunshine.

"Your auntie said I could do with a bit of vitamin D," she said. "And she was right. This is lovely."

I put the plate down and sat on a chair beside her. She was still pale and the dark circles under her eyes hadn't gone, but she seemed happier than she had been in a very long time. There was even a slight smile on her face.

"I haven't thanked you, Jake, for everything you've done for me," she said. She put her mug down. "I can't imagine how hard it must have been."

I shrugged. "It's all right," I said.

Mum reached out a hand and took mine, gripping it tightly. "No, it's not. And I promise you that nothing like this will ever happen again, OK?"

I nodded, trying not to cry. Now things were starting to feel like they were getting better I was realizing how bad they'd been. It was so nice to have that worry lifted from my shoulders and to know that Mum was getting well.

I looked over at Wilson who was rolling on his back in the damp grass making snorting noises. We laughed.

"You'd better eat that roll, Mum. Before it gets cold," I said.

She nodded and picked up the roll, taking a big bite.

"I'm going to go and check on Nina now," I said.

Mum nodded and smiled. "Give her my love," she said.

We were well into the new project Matthew, Melody and I had come up with – Operation: Look After Nina.

I rapped the knocker on the Rectory door. It took a long time, but eventually the door opened and Nina was stood there, pulling her cardigan a little tighter round herself.

"Oh, hello, Jake," she said. "Come on in."

The sparkle that had been there for a few days had gone, but she looked like she was trying to put on a brave face.

I followed her to the lounge and she sat in her armchair. Pepper leaped on to her lap and Nina stroked her soft head. After Leonard had been arrested, the neighbours had helped tidy up, putting all the things that he'd removed or damaged back where they belonged. Cameron and Kyle even found her some nice new furniture to replace the broken bits, and they'd added a lemon rug that really brightened up the lounge. I looked up at the old chandelier, which Mr Charles had cleaned himself, and it twinkled in the sunlight that was streaming through the window. I counted five empty spaces where the diamonds had hung and a few more where the glass had smashed, but it still looked good.

We sat in silence. I wasn't sure what to do or say. It was hard when someone was so sad and there was nothing you could do to make them happy again.

"They reckon Leonard is going to go to prison," I blurted out. Then I instantly regretted bringing him up.

Nina nodded.

"I don't know what's going to happen to Danny, though. It seems sad he got caught up in it all. Just because his dad was bad, doesn't mean he is," I said. After all, it was down to Danny that the police caught Leonard as he was the one who'd made the phone call.

It was then I noticed something on the mantlepiece beside the rows of Michael's trophies. It was a small square purple puzzle box. I frowned. "Did Danny leave that behind?" I asked, pointing to it.

"No. He sent it to me. Wasn't that nice of him? He's staying with his mum," said Nina, visibly cheering. "He knew how much I liked his one. It came with a little card saying he was sorry for the problems he caused. And he has stuck little notes on the squares. Have a look."

I stood up and took the puzzle box and opened it. On some of the squares were tiny stickers with little handwritten messages. I read a couple. *You are loved.* And *Danny thinks you're great!*

"It might seem strange to say it, but I think I'll keep in touch with Danny," said Nina. "I might not have my son back, but it feels like I've gained a grandson somehow."

I smiled. That was lovely. Maybe we'd end up seeing Danny again after all?

I glanced up at the shelf where the model planes that Nina's husband had made were sitting.

Nina followed my gaze and she smiled. "Oh, that reminds me. I found one of those model kits," said Nina. "Brand new and in its box. Shall we have a go?"

That sounded great to me. "Yes, please!"

I sat at the kitchen table for two hours with Nina as we fixed the pieces of plane together. Nina helped to work out which piece went where, but she said I could do the gluing as her eyesight wasn't so good. It was quite fiddly but in the end we had something that looked like a plane.

"Maybe you could come back to paint it when it's dry?" said Nina.

That was the bit I was looking forward to the most. "That'll be good," I said.

From down the hallway we heard the sound of a large vehicle coming along our road. Nina and I went to the lounge to take a look.

"That's a bit big for our road, isn't it?" she said, peering round the curtain. A huge lorry was trying to park outside number one. It went back and forth a few times, and then it shuddered as the engine was switched off.

"It looks like the new neighbours are moving in at last," said Nina. She sat back in her armchair again. I was itching to leave to see who we were getting next door and I reckoned Matthew and Melody would both be peering out of their windows now, too.

"I'm going to go now, Nina. But I'll be back soon," I said.

"That would be lovely, Jake," said Nina. "Thank you."

Out on the close, Matthew and Melody were standing on Melody's driveway, and I joined them as three men got out of the removal lorry and unlocked the big doors at the back.

"I can't believe we're going to meet our new neighbours at last!" said Melody. We looked down the road for any sign of another car but it was empty. "Where are they?"

"Maybe they're just going to put their furniture in the house and move in another day?" I said.

"No! They can't do that. I can't wait any longer," said Melody.

"They're probably moving in tomorrow instead," said Matthew. "Come on."

We were about to go our separate ways when there was the sound of a low-pitched growling motor. The sound reminded me a bit of those steam-engine contraptions you sometimes see at summer fairs. The ones that make a 'putt-putt-putt' sound with lots of smoke.

"What is that noise?" said Melody.

The three of us stared down the road as a turquoise-coloured camper van hurtled round the corner, tipping dangerously to one side.

We stared, open-mouthed, as the van thundered towards us. Country music blared out of the open windows and I saw the curtain at Mr Charles's twitch. The van took a sharp left-hand turn straight towards number one, swerving round the removals truck before screeching to a halt on the driveway. The engine spluttered off, as did the music. Mr Charles came out of his house, standing on his front door step with his arms folded.

A man wearing a bright yellow jumper, jeans and trainers got out of the driving seat of the camper van. He nodded over at Mr Charles, giving him a tip of an invisible hat.

"Afternoon, squire!" he called out.

Mr Charles didn't say a word.

The passenger door opened next, and a woman wearing a denim jacket, T-shirt and shorts got out. Her bright orange hair was piled up on her head and tied with a brown scarf. I thought she was wearing some kind of wrap round her body, but then I realized the wrap was wriggling and it was, in fact, a baby in a sling.

The door at the back of the van slid open and out tumbled two girls in matching dungarees. They looked to be around five and, as soon as their sandalled feet hit the pavement, they began to slap at each other, wailing as they did.

"Would you two give it a blooming rest!" yelled the

woman. She jiggled the baby up and down while she tried to pull the girls apart. She spotted Mr Charles staring and she quickly brushed some hair out of her eyes and smiled.

"Oh. Hello there! It's very nice to meet you," she said, almost curtseying. "We're the Campbells!"

Mr Charles's white eyebrows knitted together and his face looked like a thundercloud. He huffed and, without a word, went inside and slammed his door.

Finally another girl of about seven jumped down out of the van. She was wearing cut-off denim shorts, grubby trainers and a black T-shirt with a green alien on the front. Both her knees were bright red with scabs and she wiped her arm across her nose as she stared at us. In her hand she was holding a small pet carrier, but I couldn't see what animal was inside. Melody waved at her and the girl's lips curled up into a smile, revealing a missing tooth. She waved back, then hurried to the door of number one as the man in the yellow jumper opened it with a key from his back pocket. They all piled inside.

"There we go, folks," I said to Melody and Matthew. "It looks like the Campbells have arrived."

To be continued...

Also by
Lisa Thompson

The Goldfish Boy

A story of finding friendship when you're lonely, and hope when all you feel is fear.

The Magpie Riddle

Welcome back to Chestnut Close, whose residents may not always be exactly who they seem...

"A great cast of characters and an intriguing mystery – I loved it!"
Ross Welford, bestselling author of *Time Travelling with a Hamster*

A story of family, friendship and finding your place in the world.

"Brimming with Thompson's characteristic warmth and wisdom"
The Bookseller